Cry From Beyond

Cry From Beyond

Jonathan Fahey

AuthorHouse™ LLC
1663 Liberty Drive
Bloomington, IN 47403
www.authorhouse.com
Phone: 1-800-839-8640

© 2014 Jonathan Fahey. All rights reserved.

No part of this book may be reproduced, stored in a retrieval system, or transmitted by any means without the written permission of the author.

Published by AuthorHouse 01/10/2014

ISBN: 978-1-4817-6734-7 (sc)
ISBN: 978-1-4817-6735-4 (hc)
ISBN: 978-1-4817-6736-1 (e)

Library of Congress Control Number: 2014900630

Any people depicted in stock imagery provided by Thinkstock are models, and such images are being used for illustrative purposes only. Certain stock imagery © Thinkstock.

This book is printed on acid-free paper.

Because of the dynamic nature of the Internet, any web addresses or links contained in this book may have changed since publication and may no longer be valid. The views expressed in this work are solely those of the author and do not necessarily reflect the views of the publisher, and the publisher hereby disclaims any responsibility for them.

Tree of Life

For the dawn to make us clear to each other
Let the sun inch above the roof-tops

Let love be light that shows again
The blossom to the root.

Eavan Boland
(From; The Lost Land)

We would like to dedicate this poem
To the lost soul in this story
And to all the lost souls around the world.

—The Fahey Family—

To Martha

This book is dedicated to Martha Fahey. She became pregnant unwillingly, and therefore, suffed a silent, secret agony of her own. She could have terminated her pregnancy, or even her baby's life, given her state of anguish and trauma.

Her heroic couae in affording her child
the right to live is evident here.

In so doing, also, she may have atoned for he death of the first baby, 90 years before. It is uncanny that she may indeed be a relative o that baby's father.

Perhaps it is part of the divine plan she, in her courage and generosity, has given a new life, to replace that one, tragically lost, so many years ago.

Que sera sera.

Doe Glioria, Doe Gratias.

Introduction

For eight months, from October, 1996 to May 1997, the Fahey family of 286 Corrib Park, Galway City, Ireland, were terrorised by a Ghost / Poltergeist / Spirit in their family home. They were hostages t an invisible visitor or visitors.

They received no relief—until a sympathetic healer, Para-psychologist Sandra Ramdhanie, walked into their lives. Then, on a memorable Sunday in May 1997—deliverance, their trial was over, their joy unconfined.

Neighbours had noted that the Fahey's health had deteriorated dramatically over that period of time. They had clearly all had lost weight, pale and haggard, and had visibly aged, alarmingly. Yet some sceptics said they were bluffing and just looking for a new house!

Psychic Sandra Ramdhanie established the apparent source of the haunting. Her discovery was so shocking and unbelievable that the true account could not be told—until now! Indeed it is still with trepidation that we do so, because we are dealing with an enormous scandal here. We are talking about—infanticide, concealment and hypocrisy, involving the Irish Catholic Church ethos of 1900's—and, indeed, of today. To maintain outward respectability a life was sacrificed. The dramatis personae of this true life story are three; a baby or foetus, the mother (later to be come a nun); and one of the highest-ranking clerics of the Roman Catholic Church! Some details of dates and domicile have been altered so as to ensure anonymity.

Why did the Fahey family have to suffer for eight months before they got help? They are Catholics and their own local church and their clergy were only some hundreds of yards away from their home! The Catholic Church purports to be the one, true Church, the repository of Gods wisdom, love and mercy. Dealing with spirits is, presumably, part of the Church's work—Our lord and the Apostles dealt with spirits. Yet the Fahey's felt abandoned in their hour of need. Ironically it was a "pagan", Sandra Radiance, who helped them and saved their sanity.

One individual advised and warned the family against admitting such a person into their home, that she was sure to be an omen for evil. But the lord himself put it to His own critics in a similar situation; Can a devil cast out devils? Can an evil person do good works? And By their deeds shall you know them.

Who then performed 'good works' in this case? Who really cared about the Fahey's suffering? Who took pity on them? Again, the Lord Himself gives the answer in the parable of the good Samaritan. The Samaritan's were regarded as an outcast tribe of the Jewish nation, just as a 'pagan' healer might be seen in the eyes of the Catholic Church. The parable says that 'a Levite—a priest, walked by on the other side of the road.

Perhaps the Roman Catholic Church didn't know how to deal with the situation, apart from offering Mass? Perhaps they did their best. It was, however, a non-Catholic who resolved the problem.

Cry From Beyond

Sandra Ramdhanie established in her healing ceremony that the source of the haunting was the killing, years before, of a newborn infant boy, in a previous house, on a site close to the Fahey's present home. While such a "vision" is not definitive proof or fact in law, Sandra is convinced of its veracity. "What the psychic saw", however, revealed a shocking insight into the Roman Catholic ethos in Ireland. She uncovered a killing, a scandal and a cover-up. And all because of the need to protect at any cost the perceived public image of respectability of "Holy", Catholic Ireland", apparently? The "scandal" involved here was that one or both of the parents of the baby was a professed celibate in religious life, viz; a nun and / or a high-ranking clergyman!(A second account varies slightly). While Sandra was merely the "medium" of this discovery, and therefore it is not right to ever shoot the "messenger", she nevertheless was so shocked at this revelation that she resolved to alter the facts and dates involved so as not to identify the central characters. And because a psychic vision is not legal fact, she is not duty-bound to report a murder/ sandal. "A vision" is not vision!

It is a sad irony indeed (notwithstanding that the evidence is only a "vision") that it was because a child was born in a Catholic milieu, that it had to die. It ought never be a source of shame 'when a child is born'. In fact God said 'Increase and multiply and fill the earth' and Christ said 'Suffer (allow) little children to come on to Me'. If the baby had been born to Protestant clerics, for example, they would have been glad, even if they where unmarried. When is it ever a crime or shame to have a baby? Apparently in the Irish Catholic environment, when the parents are un married or in religious life? Thus an innocent baby died because its parents where clerics of the pro-life, holy, Catholic Irish Church!

Now, there is a disagreement as to who the killer of the baby boy.

A clairvoyant employed for this book says that it was the mother, at the behest of the father. He states that the father was _ _ _ _ _ _ _ _ _ _ an Archbishop! The psychic "saw" a Bishop!?

But the mother did not kill the child, according to Sandra. In her vision she saw a lay-man.(the father, brother of the young nun, she believes) suffocate the baby boy. The nun did not aid or abet him. It would seem that this man was so overcome with shame because of the prevailing "respectable" Catholic ethos, that he felt he couldn't risk waiting to have the baby adopted, lest the sandal visited upon his family's reputation would be discovered before then. Such was the insidious power of the Catholic Church ethos over the minds of the people that apparently he felt, in terror, that he had to act immediately. What a dilemma that man faced. He knew of the Commandment" "thou shall not kill", he knew of hell and eternal damnation. Yet, his fear before the perceived standard of the Catholic respectability outweighed even the awful prospect of Hells—fire for the murder of that baby boy. What anguish he must have suffered. And what a perversion of a nation's moral principles and mores that drove him to it? Unless he was a cold, calculating killer, he couldn't have been responsible for his actions. Perhaps he knew this and trusted in God's mercy and understanding. If he were a protestant he would not have suffered this awful trauma and would not have felt he had to kill and hide in a shame. So then, is the Irish Catholic ethos responsible for the killing in this instance—and in any others? And did the Fahey family suffer because of the moral mores of their own Church? Or is this whole "vision" a fantasy?

Cry From Beyond

In a second check, the clairvoyant says that the female parent was later a mother of a nun, and was ordered to abort by the Archbishop.

All of this conjecture however, because it is based on a "vision" and is therefore not a statement of actual legal fact. Therefore, while the events as "seen" by Sandra will not be set in their true context here, both in place and time, names will not be given. After all this a "vision" and must therefore be deemed, in the absence of concrete, empirical evidence, a story more of fantasy and fiction that of fact?

It is significant that the clairvoyant's account is at variance with the above. He states that the mother killed the child, or aborted. Again, this is not be taken as definitive, verily or legally. Couldn't the infant have been still born? Or just died naturally! The gravity of the haunting experience would suggest a very violent death at this person hands. Sandra says that the mother of the murdered baby boy had a another child a girl watch became a Nun. Many years later.

N.B No murder charges was ever preferred in this case, as no public revelation was made. It was a secret, covert operation, in the 1900's. It was perhaps a forced abortion? Sandra, however, says that event was not the direct the direct cause of the Fahey's haunting.

Genesis

In the beginning, an ordinary farmhouse stood on open land in the vicinity of the present Fahey family home at 286, Corrib park, Newcastle, Galway City, Ireland. While the land remained in use of its owner the house was rented to alternate tenants during the early 1900's. One such family, the central one of this story, had an only child, a daughter, who became a nun. Now, by coincidence, it is believed that another family who lived there at different time, also had, in this case, two daughters (of a family of four children) in the nuns. The family at the heart of this story is the former, the one with an only child. The proliferation of religious vocations at this time is not too surprising, as many Irish Catholic Families aspired to having a son or daughter "In the cloth".

While psychologist Sandra Ramdhnie "felt" that Druidic rituals may have occurred long, long ago in this area, she fixes the "prime-mover" of the Fahey story in events of the 1900's at the farmhouse. The daughter and only child of this family was a nun. She became pregnant—by a dignitary of the Irish Roman Catholic Church. That man was, in fact an Archbishop or Bishop! A member of the hierarchy of the Irish Catholic Church!

Sandra has described his appearance, but has not named him, nor the location of his Seed in Ireland. It is not the purpose here to identify individuals. Besides, the baby, when born, was killed, but not by his father. The Bishop, father of the child, is now dead many, many years. The mother of the child also.

A neighbour son of the owner of the land in the 1900's say that the farmhouse became haunted at that time, and this possibly accounts for the frequent changeover of tenancy there. The land was sold and the house demolished to make way for the construction of the Galway Corporation housing estate of Corrib Park around 1970-1972 ("Corrib" is the name of Galway's lake and main river). Now, it would seem that the ghost (s) became dormant or inactive for over 90 years, and all during the Fahey's occupancy of the new house on the site, I.e., no.286, Jckie and Esther Fahey own two children were born when the family lived for a time elsewhere. (Micheal and sister Martha). The Ghost re-awaken when Martha Fahey, in 1996, brought hereown child home from the maternity hospital and while the neighbours were opening up the wall of their own home (adjoining the Fahey's home) for an extension. So, either the new baby or the house extension wall-opening triggered the haunting, it would seem. (Micheal and Martha were not "incarnated", because they lived elsewhere as babies.)

Does this mean that Martha's baby Sarah-Louise is the re-incarnation of the murdered "spirit-baby" which was haunting the house? Sarah-Louise continually "saw" the other baby and played with him/ her. The Fahey's believed that there was an adult "presence" also (footsteps, violence,etc,) which was malign, but "saw" only one spirit there,I.e. a baby, and she says it was benign. She did not feel any "evil" in the house. She believed that the spirit-baby only sought the same love and sense of belonging enjoyed by baby Sarah from her mother,and became violent only when ignored or deprived of mother-love. "All you need is love" song by the Beatles, and love is the essence of God and ture religion. When Sandra conducted a "love-in" healing ceremony the spirit-baby felt loved and wanted, and "passed on" smiling and joyous in a ray of golden sunlight, rising through the ceiling. And Sarah cired bitterly at the losing of little play-mate.

Principal Characters

The Fahey family—Jackie and Esther in their 40's
Michael and Martha—Their children

"Sheila", Michael ex Fiancee (who asked for name to changed)

Sarah—Louise—Jackie and Esther's Grandchild
the heart of the unfolding of the story.

Sandra Radiance—Para—pyschologist, the healer. Patrick and Valerie Lee—Neighbours and true friends

Chapter One

The Visitation

Jackie and Esther Fahey have a son and a daughter, Michael and Martha, Michael and his fiancee at the time "Sheila",which they had plans to marry in 20001. This is "Sheila's" account:

It started with a smell in the house in November, 1996. The Local Authority checked for leaking gas, ect.,but found nothing. Michael described the smell as of rotting flesh or meat and strong smell of urine. It lasted for over a month.(It is now know that a murdered baby's body was buried on that site in the 1900's)

'One night, at about 3.45 a.m. we were wakened by a beam of intense light entering our room via the window. It lasted for five minutes and faded slowly. We were frightened and sat there in silence, motionless. We concluded that there must be some logical explanation. Next day we were departing down the country for the lon holiday weekend. Before we left Esther was vacuum-cleaning Michael's room when she found egg-shells scattered all over the floor. Jackie had been painting the ceiling so Esther, at first, thought it was flakes of paint.We didn't worry and all headed off happily on our weekend "safari".

'On our return on Monday morning we again found egg-shells on the floor. We decided to keep them for examination. The shells continued to appear for weeks and they increased in size and number. Then we began to hear strange noises outside of our room, on the landing. We wondered if there was something sinister afoot. At frist we two were the only ones to hear anything, and always between 1 a.m. and 3 a.m. We were always last to bed and were light sleepers.

'Martha was a heavy sleeper and at first didn't wake or hear the noises-and footsteps! When she did begin to notice the nightly sounds we became more concerned and the three of us joined together in vigils in front of the Tv in the sitting room.

On one occasion it was just Michael and I, watching TV. We heard a noise coming from baby Sarha's room overhead. We thought that it might be Martha checking on her child. Ten minutes later we heard someone come down the stairs and walk down the hall. I asked Mike (Michael) to look but he said no. I opened the door and there was Martha, in white night dress, and with a pale and blank expression. She had heard peculiar noises upstairs and had come down to join us. She had not checked in on baby Sarah. It was now about 3.30 a.m. Esther and Jackie, who slept downstairs were woken by our sounds and joined us briefly, believing that any noises were just floor-boards creaking, etc. Although the noises and footsteps continued nightly we didn't at first think of anything paranormal or sinister.

'On one particular evening Mike and I went to the cinema. On our return at midnight we were meet by a young girl, a neighbour. Jackie and Esther were away and Martha had been alone with Sarah. The girl told us that Martha had run out of the house screaming and was afraid to go back. The girl said that Martha had been watching

TV at 10 p.m. when she heard a strange thumping noise from the babby's room overhead. She hurried upstairs but couldn't open the door, as if a strong force was perventing her access. Baby Sarha was hysterical, crying and screaming. Martha repeatly tried to open the door. She had finally run, screaming, into the street, calling for help.

'A neighbour accompanied her back in and up the stairs. This time the bedroom door opened. Sarha face was etched with fear, with tears on her cheeks. But Martha was afraid to stay and had called in this girl to babysit. We thanked the girl and told her that we would take over.

'The frist thing I did was to check on the baby. She was asleep and looked peaceful, as if nothing had happened. I did, however, feel a distinct coldness in the room. As I passed the bathroom/toilet with its door open, the toilet flushed on its own. I was now really frightened. I decided to take Sarah downstairs and keep her with us. Just then she woke with an unearthly crying that filled the whole house. I held her close trying to comfort her. I was sure then that there was something terribly wrong, and most of all I felt that I was being watched.

'Downstairs we decided to phone for help and to tell Martha to come home. But Mike couldn't get though to any number, even 999. All the while he said that there was a foot-tapping sound beside him, as if someone was warning him to stop. H looked white and drained. We felt the temperature drop,like a cold breeze wafting through. Then a loud thump from the fireplace and Sarha's baby picture was upturned on the floor. It was terrifying.I felt that we were in the presence of something sinister indeed. I began crying and laughing simultaneously. Mike went to gather Sarha's clothes and things, leaving me alone in the sitting room. Suddenly a silver picture frame was lifted from its place and hovered in front of me, before smashing into shards against the fireplace. I tried to scream but no sound came. Mike came back in and saw me terror-stricken. We decided to get out. I grabbed my bag and car keys and left with Sarha,as another crash was heard. I didn't dare look back, but Mike did and saw the coffee table upturned on the floor.

'We drove off to collect Martha. Sarha sat quietly in Mike's arms, knowing that her sleep had been disturbed yet again. After a long silence Mike spoke to me, wide-eyed"

"You know, back there, as I was closing the door of the house, some powerful force pushed and slammed the door after me".

'We knew, instinctively that our house must be haunted and that we could not return there. But Martha said that she needed more stuff for the baby, a quick visit would do.

'On our return we found a gathering of neighbours outside the house they had heard the commotion. They offered us accommodation but we felt that we had to get as far away as possible. Jackie and Esther were down in Waterford with relatives for a few days. We decided to go and join them even at 2 a.m. We drove out of Corrib Park, to the consternation of our neighbours, intending never to return to that dreaded house.

'It was almost daylight when we reached Waterford, some 140 miles away. A neighbour in Galway then phoned to see if we were alright, and old us that the lights in the house had been flashing on and off periodically all night,as if the place were occupied.

'After so many sleepless nights at home, we were glad of this respite in Waterford, where, exhausted and jaded we were able to rest and sleep well into the day. But we knew that we had to return to Galway. Jackie phoned neighbours to see what was happening? They said that strange things had been occurring ; lights flashing, furniture being thrown, curtains left open by us, now closed, on the front room window, and most eerily of all, a baby's crying, audible and piercing.

'After a few days rest, we all returned together to Galway. We had to return to the house, at least initially. We decided to sleep all together in he sitting room floor, but we all slept dressed, and with belongings packed. That first night passed uneventfully. Jackie and Esther had to go to work, but Esther was sent home. She looked like she had aged 10 years and she was the one most affected psychologically. We worried about her health.

'Mike got a call from R.T.E radio1, the main national station. He told the whole harrowing the tale over the airwaves. The story gripped the nation and listeners continued calling in with their own accounts expressing sympathy. The presenter asked Mike to phone the next day if anything happened that night.

'All was quite until around 2.45 a.m. Sarha began to cry as if someone was hurting her, and we couldn't comfort her. We noticed that her teddies and toys had been arranged in a circle about her cot, something a small child would do. We were troubled indeed, but felt somewhat relieved in that we had an audience arranged with the Roman Cathlic Bishop of Galway, Dr.McLoughlin, in the atfernoon. We felt that he could help us out.

'In the morning Mike was first into the bathroom, He found that all the tops of the bottles and tubes had been removed and piled in a heap in the bath, again, as if done by a child at play.

Jackie and Mike met the Bishop, He was friendly and welcoming and not at all surprised at events in our home. He saithat he would arrange for a mass in the house, butthat was all he could do; he had made it clear that it was not a matter easy to resolve. That evening at 6.30 a priest called. He blessed Sarah and the home and said he would return on Tuesday, May 6th to say mass. That night a sence of terror gripped us, huddled together, in the sitting room. Only Sarah slept.

During the following days Mike was on the National radio again. Once more we were swamped with phone calls but no one offered any solution to our on going nightmare. The Mass as arranged for the 6th of May, 1997 and we invited as many neighbours as possible, believing in the greater power of collective prayer. The local radio station were covering the event too, set for 6 p.m. Newspaper reporters were arriving also. As the Mass time approached, Jackie went upstairs to place holy relics in baby Sarah's room. He found the place in a mess, everything scattered in disarray. It was as if the haunting-presence in the house did not want the Mass to proceed. Sarah was downstairs the the rest of us, and there was nobody else to make this mess up in the room.

'when the priest arrived and saw the crowd he said;, "Family only", and left. Sadly.we had to ask friends and neighbours to leave. One person suggested saying the Rosary for the benefit before they all left. This was done. The priest returned at around 7 p.m. and repared for the Mass in the sitting room. He blessed each of us that were there. As the Massbegan it was apparent that the priest was extremely nerous. His hands shook and he's voice carried a certain quiver. During the Massa child's crying began upstairs in the baby's room, clearly audible. The priest gradually raised his voice and quickened his delivery.

'He continually referred to Sarah as "little boy". After Mass we spoke to him about the crying. He didn't say he heard it, yet he was pale and his voice trembled.

'All he could say to us, repeatedly, was; "there's no human explanation for this".Everyone was downstairs during the Mass, so the crying is unexplained.

We felt no reassurance or relief after the Mass, and that niht we resolved to sleep all together in the sitting-room, still afraid to venure above. Next day, May 7th, our local parish priest, Fr. Hallinan, came and celebrated Mass, and blessed the home for us too.

Jackie; At 1p.m. the next day we decided to put a tape-recorder in Sarah's room, Mike put it on the bed as we were heading downstairs we heard a loud thump, Martha and Sheila ran and locked themselves into the bahtroom and the screams out them, Mike tried to get into the bathroom but he just couldn't no matter how hard he tried.

Sheila; When we saw that someone was trying to get in we thought that it was the ghost so we pushed against the door. Jackie and Mike thought that we were trapped and tried to shove the door in—they hadn't spokn at first. After we got out of the bathroom, we went to investigate the noise in from the child's room. Mike had left the recorder on the bed but it was now on the floor, a good bite across the room away from the bed but undamaged.The frightening thing about this the Ghost didn't want us to record it was if the ghost was reading our thought's. Surely this was an adult presence? If so, who? At 11.20 p.m. we were all together in the front room, when we heard a child's crying overhead and Sarah's lullaby system playing, yet Sarah was with us in the front room, asleep, and nobody upstairs?

'Next there was a terrifying baby's wail upstairs, Jackie turned white and shuddered, Martha screamed, I cried, Esther just was glued to the spot. Jackie bravely ran upstairs into the childs room, but everything stopped suddenly. On his way down the wailing started again. He went back up—and silence!

We all decided to investigate, in Sarah's room. On our way upstairs I saw an object lift and hurl against the baby's door with such force that fragments landed at the bottom of the stairs, I screamed and turned, twisting my ankle and falling to the bottom of the stairs. I was petrified with fear. The vessel which smashed was a ceramic jug which was on a small table on the landing.

We all rushed from the house, some screaming, we meet the neighbours outside, they had heardb the dis turbance. Jackie, Mike and I decided to vist a religious man who lived nearby. He wanted to enter the house with blessed candles and to say some prayers. We knew that the ghost (s) did not like religious relics and we advised him not to enter. That night we slept in the neighbours. The next morning everyone looked haggard, pale and drawn. For the first time Jackie and Esther truly understood the terror what we all went though and experienced on the Saturday night before.

We concluded that this was it, we were finished with this house. We went back to tidy up and pack our clothes.

Jackie phoned the radio programme to tell them our ordeal. Phone calls came from far and near and keeped on calling.

Jackie and Esther then went into town to ask the Local Authorites for alternative accommodation. They received no help whatsoever and returned angry and despondent. They were close to depair, their whole world shatted. Esther was particularly badly affected psychologically and was not eating at all. She sobbed continuosly. Even stoical Martha had a gaunt and haunted look.

All during Thursday phone calls came and requests for interviews. Many were well-wishers too. On that afternoon a lady journalist (Aideen Sheehan) and a photographer froa Dublin newspaper (Evening Herald) arrived.

She seemed totally sceptical however. But her views would be soon change. She asked if she could stay in the house with us that night.

That night there was noises upstairs, footsteps and thumps, but she said she didn't really hear anything. At 11pm Sarah woke suddenly, crying and screaming—always an omen. Her clothes had been moved. We were frightened but this time, with the reporter present we were determined to brave it and stay in the house, if possible. All was quiet again for some time. Around 3.35a.m we felt the room go cold. I sensed that there was someone else in the room, so we left the front room, before we heard a thundering crash there. I ran, screaming, into the kitchen, where the reporter was sitting typing up her account. We looked at each other in fear. Hesitantly we edged towards the front room. The place was wrecked. One of Sarah's favourite objects, a large, two—foot long ceramic dog on the hearth had been shattered to dust. The T.V. had moved, ornaments and pictures scattered. The reporter turned over a silver-framed picture, then dropped it an recoiled. The picture was of the Nativity with Mary, Joseph and baby Jesus. Phrhaps this had nuaunces of the source of the haunting? Religious images play an obvious part in this story. It seems that the spirit baby or other ghost(s) did not like them?

When the reporter saw the scattered state of the front room she was obviously perturbed but put on a brave face. However, in her newspaper article later (see same) she described it as her "Night of terror" in a "haunted house".

After that incident we were convinced that it wasn't safe to stay in the house. The reporter packed her gear and together we, once again, went to our neighbours. It was 4a.m. at 5a.m. we tried to get some sleep but all through the reporter kept relaying her story to H.Q. for that days edition. At 6.30 a.m. Her collegaue returned. He was in state of disbelief when he saw the destruction in the front room. He took photographs and they left for the early train back to Dublin, a chastened pair, I wouls say.

Esther and Jackie were grievously troubled, realising we would definitely have to leave thir home. Esther was crying and sobbing; "my house is gone, my house is gone".

At 9 0'clock the following morning I phoned R.T.E. radio and told the presenter the story of the nights events. We received lots of letters also from people concerned about us. Mass bouquets too. For the next few days we had widespread media coverage, newpapers, T.V. crews, local and national radio, an English T.V. station expressed an interest in our story and asked for an interview. A localRoman Catholic Franciscan priest phoned saying he would like to visit us. He came at 5 p.m. It was a comfort and a relief when he said that he believed us. Ours was not the only mysterious tale he had heard. He told us of an occasion when he had a bottle of holy water in a room; the bottle was invisibly taken and smashed on the floor. Again, in a room, he had witnesseda shower of stone and fire start spontaneously. That night (Friday) was quiet, we slept at the neighbours house again.

We checked the house on Saturday morning and notced the baby's room window open and one of her toys out on the landing? Back at the neighbours house Jackie had observed that ther was a burn-mark from a holy medal (of Our Lady) on her chest (Sarah's).

We were all greatly disturbed and frightened, and concerned for Sarah.

The phone rang—it was a tridentate priest wanting to help. Wetold him about the medal. He asked us al to gather around the phone while he blessed us. He asked then to put the phone to Sarah's ear. She became very agitated, but after the priest said some Latin prayers, she gradually became calm and peaceful.

Later he told us while praying on the phone, he's hair stood up on the back of his neck. He asked us to bring the baby to him, in the midlands. On the way there, Jackie felt ill, Mike got a smothering sensation, Sarah was crying, I (Sheila) found driving very difficult. Certain obstacles got in our way even though we knew the road, as if the spirit didn't want us to rech our destination. When we met him he told us to sprinkle holy water and salt in the rooms at our home. We felt very unsure and uncomfortable about this cleric, and returned ome as soonas possible.

Saturday, May 11th, 1997; When we got back, there was a lady with two reporters waiting for us. She had seen us the T.V. and was concerned about our distraught state, especially Esther. She introduced herself as **Sandra Ramdhaine,** an Anglo-Indian lady from Dublin, and a para-psychologist by profession.

She spoke briefly to each of the family and performed a preliminary healing on young Sarah and told Martha that her child was not in physical danger.

N.B,; On another occasion, Mike and I decided to pray. As we recited Mike felt a choking, suffocating sensation around his throat, as if some force were trying to stop him. Was this a re-enactment of the baby's death?

P.S; When the burn mark of the holy medal appeared on Sarah's body, the family took a close-up photograph, as evidence. But when the film was developed, no marks!?

Chapter Two

Deliverence/Exodus

Sandra had said that she would return the next day, Sunday, at 3 p.m.that night was peaceful and quite, because of the healing. Sandra duly arrived as agreed, and with her were two journalists. She asked Esther to take Sarah next door because she wanted to talk to Martha about Sarah's dad and something about he's background and whether there was any likelihood of a curse being placed on the baby. Martha told her; no. She next went upstairs with the journalists and shortly afterwards called Mike up. They joined in placing candles and incense all around the house. This was o balance the energies of the poltergiest so that we could control the spirit-entity. Sheplaced her hands on the wall and telepathically connected with entity. She asked everyone then to gather around in a circle and imagine that the spirit-baby was in her arms. She placed the spirit-baby in the middle of the circle on the floor. We all joined hands and Sandra told us to imagine with eyes closed the baby on the floor. She gave us some relaxation exercises to perform. She then told Martha to sit in the middle of circle and imagine she was holding the spirit-baby in her arms and for us to imagine the same, eyes closed.

At this time everyone imagined a different scene of the spirit-baby's trasportation. One saw a holy figure holding the child, while anothers saw a child in grey clothes disappear in a strong beam of light. Mike saw a baby wrapped in white swaddling clothes and swathed in bright light. While everyone's vision was different yet similar, they all experienced one thing in common—agreat feeling of peace, serenity and happiness, as if a great weight had been lifed from us all. For the first time in eight monyhs everyone felt happy again. The house felt peaceful that night and there was a tangible glow of warmth where there had been an unearthly chill.

When the ceremony was over everyone breathed an unbelievable sigh of relief. Sandra told us that the spirit had gone over to the other side, peacefully, and without hostility. We were then and we still are entirely indebated to Sandra for our deliverance. From the moment we met her we knew that she was special. We expected to see a gypsy-type dark haired lady in long robes and flowing tresses. Instead we met a blonde-haired lady with leather trousers. She wore a beautiful cross around her neck which was bought in Tunisia (although she is not a Christian).She was warm, friendly and kind and we instinctively knew that she would help us. She empathised an sympathised with us in our terrible hour of need.

After the ceremony Sandra placed pieces of rose quartz around the house so as to make it uncomfortable for other spirits to enter the house. The reporters were deeply affected too by what they had witnessed and they quietly bade farwell and set off to meet their newspapers deadline's.

Sandra, on the other hand, sat around discussed the happenings and the background of the spirit-baby. What she was about to tell us was quite a shock indeed. So shocking that we decided to relate a different account to the public at the time. That was that a baby had been born to a priest and a nun and that the baby had been smothered and buried under-floor, 90 years ago (It was in fact a Bishop! Yes a Bishop)

Sandra explained that the pungent smell in the house was that of the rotting flesh of the dead baby, re-visited paranormally. The reason why only family members could get the smell she called clairsentience, similar to clairvoyance.

While we were gathered together with Sandra there was a knock at the door. It was a man and a young woman and they said they had a story about the old farm house and the occupants, on which site our present house now stood:

Many years ago a relative of his had owned the farmland here and as a boy he'd worked on the land. He remembered the farm house clearly. It was being rented to tenants, and he knew of some families who had come and gone there. One family had a child, a daughter, who later became a nun. We were all stunned when he mentioned a nun, because Sandra had just told us her "nun's story". Too good to be a coincidence, we all thought. And almost unbelievable too that the dead baby's parents were avowed celibate religious, and more aware. Presumably, than most, of the commandments; "thou shalt not kill".

While it is not alleged who actually killed the baby, it is undoubted that in the Catholic ethos of the day, the shame of extra-marital sex—for religious, couldn't be countenanced, such was the fear of the strictures of the Catholic Church that, apparently, muder was a preferable option to the parenting of a beautiful, innocent, human baby!

The man added that the farmhouse had been haunted, with strange happenings witnessed there. The immediate area was barren, nothing would grow, and birds and animals would come near. The occupants had gone through the same terrors as us, e.g., blankets being pulled off a person in bed, and the sounds of a child crying, and objects being thrown about the house and rooms. Tenants kept leaving and eventually nobody would live there at all, so the farmhouse fell into disrepair and had to be knocked down.

When we first meet Sandra she asked if there was any building work going on or lately? Martha remembered that when she come home with the baby from the hosiptal she remembered giving out about the work going on next door it washard for the new born and Martha to get sleep. Sandra felt that perhaps childs spirit was trapped in the walls for years and felt unloved and rejected. When baby Sarah arrived the spirit-nbaby my have been energised and have "twinned" with Sarah, in order to seek Martha's love and affection. The spirit-baby may also have been jealous of the attention given to Sarah. We firmly believe that Sarah saw

And played with the ghost-child. She would began to make unusual sounds all of a sudden and swould kick and laugh as if she were playing with Martha-but this would be when she was by her self, she would also stare and be transfixed at one spot, and even when you'd lift her up or turn her away from the spot she would let of the louds crys until you placed her back to the spot she was lying in and she'd stop and start smiling and kicking and baby talking. Sandra felt that when the ghost-baby saw Martha was not giving it the same love and attention that when it would throw toys around and started waking Sarah from her sleep at night and we all in the family had our things moved caps removed of creams etc, photo's moved of walls but nothing ever belonging to Martha, We asked Sandra about this "Martha was the one unwitting souce of the child haunting".

12th of May, 1997, Sandra left in the evening (Sunday) and we thanked her from our hearts for the wonderful deliverane she had wrought. She assured us that the vistation was appeased and that we would have no more suffering. Yet, our terror had been such that we still afraid to sleep inour own beds. So we all huddled together again that night in the front room, the cold chill had gone from the house and everyone felt unburdened and relaxed. Everything was silent that night. Only the faint scent of incense and rose-quartz betrayed any prior occurrence. And for the first time young Sarah slept the whole night-great relief for us all.

Monday morning wasvery busy; an overseas T.V. station was coming over to do a documentary;Sandra arrived back with a present for Sarah—a soft-toy dog, to replace the porcelain fireplace dog which left this world in a bang.

Sandra had made a great impression on us all. She was a pure lady, and someone even though she was out of pocket and received no money from us at all. The newspaper's continued to call, as did the radio stations. We were now trying to get back to **normal** life. It would take time o reconcile the terrible ordeal we had been through.We will never forget but we hope that we will learn to accept. It will always be with us. Every noise and bump will suggest an unearthly echo. But if we ever should doubt our experiences, all we have to do is look at those newspaper cuttings and our haunting, pale and pained expressions,and of that hell is on earth we suffered in the year 1996-'97.Yet there are many people who don't believe. We believe because we've lived it all them months.

Blessed are those who have not seen, yet believe, most of all blessed are the merciful—blessed are the peace-makers Sandra, who ook pity on our family and delivered us, Amen.

Extract from the Mirror, May 13th, 1997;

Sandra,who has been called on to banish a spook for top broadcaster Gay Byrne,(Late Late Show the longest running talk show in Ireland) carried out a ceremony to "rebalance the energies" in the Fahey' Home. She gathered the family and friends in circle around Martha. Then she asked them to visualise the ghost child being filled with "golden sunlight" and moving peacefully out of the house. She lit special incense sticks from Tibet and burned whitesage used by American native Indians to purify the two-storey terraced house. She also "sealed off" the house against spirits using mixture herbs and salts. Sandra said "I tried to make it an uncomfortable place for ghosts". She added ; "This was a fascinating case with several unusual factors. I contacted the spirits which was haunting the Fahey's home and asked how it died as a child. These spirits usually have traumatic or violent deaths. I Learned in telepathic communication that this spirit was a baby born to a young woman and a clergyman. I thought she was a young nun.

Chapter Three

Witnessing

Jackie Fahey; When growing up one always heard tales of ghosts and banshees. It was believed by some that the banshee ("bean siodh", Gaelic) or fairy-witch would herald by wailing/kneening the death of a person in the house hold. Animals, too, could see ghosts, almost everyone knew of a haunted house. Little did In know or expect that one day it would be—my own house that people would be talking about.!

The on set of our particular "Visitation" was the **Smell** a smell so foul and putrid that I had difficulty breathing, and actually used an inhaler's. Then the haunting itself. We turned to Church for help but unfortunately received little help or understanding, yes they did arrange the mass at the house, but that was ineffective. We were left to "bear our cross" alone.

Our next recourse was the Local Authorities, Seeking another house, again an inability to help immediately. All the while our health, mental as well physical, was deteriorating. Everyone said that they could see that I'd aged over the long months. Our real salvation was one person, one woman-Sandra Ramdhanie, a para-psychologist, an

Anglo-Indian lady living in Dublin. She confirmed the existence of a poltergeis or ghost and said she could put it to rest. She visualised physically that a new born baby had been strangled on this site, when a previous cottage existed here by my house was here. The body was buried underneath the floorboards of the old farm house. Both parents were in religious life, she thought. When one Roman Catholic clergyman heard of Sandra's success he dismissed it as a "pagan act" and even suggested that we may have imagined the whole thing. No mention at all of our suffering, or a remedy.

The media were helpful in highlighting our cause. This led to finding our saviour—Sandra. Our home is now very peaceful, things are back to normal. I wonder, Yet can life ever be the same again?

(**N.B.**On the lighter side; late one night(1 a.m) there was a knock on the front door. It was a really drunk lad wishing to call to see the haunted house and totalk about the ghost he was light hearted guy and he said he'd needed to have the drink in him for some **dutch courage . . .** funny ramdom or what?

Mike Fahey;—for a long, long time I wondered if we would ever be happy again, given the nightmare we experienced, and feeling of desolation and emptiness. We were afraid to sleep in our own beds, in our own house. I feared that my Mother, Esther, especially, would suffer a nervous breakdown. Yet there are people who think that this was all an elaborate hoax—for publicty or a new house. Is a new house worth all that suffering? Anyway, we are now living happily in that same house our home. Would any of our critics have lived in our house? Would they have swapped places with us? If not, why not? There is an old West Indian saying; Do not criticise a man, until you have first walked a mile in his mocassins. Any takers?

Saturday evening May 1997, My dad got a phone call from a student in Dublin asking if he might be permitted to try out his video equipment in our house, in the hope of recording something. He arrived on the following evening. He said he was compiling a programme for T.V. He set up the camera and Dictaphone in the baby's room, didn't get capture anything, even though we could hear the baby crying, and breathing noises on the landing. It was like the ghost did not wish to give up it's story. At about 12.30 one Thursday nighta couple called to our house to relate their own account of a haunting. They said that it started when their youngest daughter passed aged just 3 years old. The house became cold, even with a blazing fire down. They had to leave when things were being broken and smashed. This was a story not unlike our story here at the house. Perhaps their young child had been neglected or felt unloved and aggrieved.

Another phone call in May 1997 came from a college person in Galway,an experton the paranormal. He thought that he could help us. He had come where temperature fluctuations were felt. It was found that the house was built on a graveyard. They had to get a priest to perform an exorcism.

Again, an older woman called, saying that she was a spiritualist and could ri us of our ghost, (s). It could be done with a lot of prayer. Nothing came of it however, But we where grateful for her call anyway.

An hotel manageress in Galway told me of a haunted hotelin the north west of Ireland where she had worked. She discovered that the place had a gruesome secret. A family once lived there who had a deformed baby. They cared for him for a while but when he was two years they locked him in the attic, where he eventually died. The haunting is benign and continuing. Staff and guest tolerate it, that the ghost is harmless.

Martha Fahey;

Everyone said that I was the coolest one In the house, and perhaps I was. But I was not rational or thinking straight during the whole terrible episode. It is difficult now to believe that all this happened in our home. We were, and still are, an ordinary family. No pagan worshipping inour house. The scepitics said that my brother Mike stereo system couldn't have played on it's own,well,we weren't there, the neighbours heard it. And it hasn't got a timer, didn't have a cd, and was not switched on?

While I was in the mainly unaffected, my dad and my mum nearly cracked up. At times it seemed as if Sarah was playing with another child ghost baby friend. She would get very engrossed one place on the ceiling as if was following something or could see something that was friendly. On the day Sandra conducted the healing and the baby-spirit "moved" on. Sarah was extremely agitated and cranky and inconsolable. It was as if she missed the company of the other baby,her friend and playmate. Even now, though the haunting is over we are still experiencing trauma. We are still wary subconsciously, continually looking and listening for the unknow o come knocking or banging around again. We probably always will, we will have to bear that mark of sorrow for the lost unkown child robbed of it's life. R.I.P. little one.

Esther Fahey—The Ghost I lived with;

This is my account of my eight months of hell—and haunting. I feared that I would lose my family and my mind. My little grand—daughter had a relic-medal—mark burned onto her chest, and this Latin-praying "Bishop" came on the phone saying that she was possessed and to bring her down to him immediately. We drove 70 miles to the midlands to see "bishop". He gave us a blessing and said that everything would be alright now. He told us not to let Sandra anywhere near our house, at her type well end bring worse things In to our lifes and home.

When we got back to galway, Sandra was waiting. What now? My husband said to let her in. she was real lady and very nice. We talked fo a half an hour. She said that I looked so bad on TV that she pitied us and came down from Dublin to offer us help. She said she wouldn't do anything that evening (Saturday 11/05/97) except take energies out of the house, and call back the next day. Strange, that was quiet one in the 8months, we still slept next door, just incase.

On Sunday Sandra arrived at 2 p.m. Thank God that she came back. I owe that lady my sanity. When it was all over, I felt so happy. But still my home will never truly feel thr same. I hope that this account will be of some help to others in ou situation; that if your mind and hearts are open there's people like Sandra willing to help you because they have the know how.

Strangely, my daughter Martha, who was so impervious to trauma during the haunting, is now o scared to stay in the house, even in the daytime. My grand-daughter, Sarah-Louise, sometimes she would say grandad about the man in the ceiling light looking down at her. But to Mike she says it's a baby. She will not go to the bathroom upstairs on her own even still.

Sarah—Louise,

I'm writing this on behalf of my grand child, at the age of four years old she woud talk about the man n the light, and been bold and taken her toys and that would make her sad grandad she would say. Now she is ten years old and I don't ask her anything she might remember about the ghost, Sandra said it's best to leave to bring it up herself.

They called to see us and she started talking about the still man or boy that play with the light and I rang Sandra said this common that as she gets old more could come out but let it come at own time.

She also remarked thather playmate never ment her any harm at all and it was lonely and unloved.

Sarah also said that he's name was called Jonathan. Which is nice to know that's what my grand-daughter make me very proud.

Jackie (continued):

Since our own story, I've been told many similar tales of the supernatural;

A woman phoned to relate the following-her home was haunted and because of her fear she got a dog for company. One morning as she came downstairs she heard him whining in his basket and trembling nervously. His back was broken, and he had to be humanely put to sleep. They discovered there used to to be a hanging gallows on the site of their home, and that priests had been hanged there during Penal Law times (18th) c. So, is our haunting a re-enactment of a previous phenomenon? We think so.

Valerie Lee—Next door Neighbour-;

I couldn't believe my eyes when Mike, Martha, (Sheila),and Baby Sarah came running out of their house at 2a.m. on May 4th 1997, screaming and shouting. They said that they would have to leave their house and go down to Waterford, where their parents were visiting family there. My mother and I tried to dissuade them, considering the unearthly hour of the night, butthey were hysterical. I really couldn't believe that anyone could be so traumatised. We tried to talk them out of going, but they said that they wanted to join their family and anyway couldn't stay in the house.

The car took off like a rocket. I didn't sleep any more that night because I went out on the street with neighboyrs, watching the house. Lights were flashing on and off and we could hear noises as well. We too were frightened and I don't think that any of slept at all that night.

The Fahey's had kept the repeating;

"Our house is haunted, there is a ghost in there". I was very worried for the family, for their sanity. When they returned we tried to help as best we could and make them comfortable in our house.We made beds for them in our sitting room and gave them dinner, etc., when needed.

I will never forget what happened, and I hope that it never occurs again. Some people refuse to believe, but seeing is believing, and I saw—and heard! I have seen how that family suffered and how it has changed their lives. Even though our family didn't experience their terror and anguish, we all felt that we shared in the events with them.

Jonathan Fahey

Patrick Lee—Neighbour—Valerie is his sister;

I live two doors away at 288 Corrib Park, Galway City. On that fateful Saturday night (May 4th, 1997), I was outside my house at about 12.30 a.m. when Mike and Sheila came running out of their house. Sheila was shouting: "Come on, lets get out, that the house has gone mad". Martha follwed with the baby Sarah. They drove off.

At about 1.15 a.m. they returned, to get some more clothes for the baby. Martha and Sarah were crying. Mike and Sheila dashed into the house and two minutes later came out running, swithing off all the lights. They took off at speed for the south of Ireland and to the rest of their family. At this stage all of the neighbours were out, having heard the commotion.

After 20 minutes the lights started flashing on and off and music began to play. Bundy, their dog, was barking all night long and next day. My dad asked me to go over the wall and feed him. As I was putting his food in the bowl

I looked up at the back of the kitchen. I saw a halo of light fill the room, so briht and unnatural that I became frightened. I leapt back over the wall and ran in home.

After that weekend and the Fahey's returned from Waterford, 136 miles away. But things got even worse for them. They had to sleep with us, but they didn't really sleep at all—for weeks and months. They looked like ghosts themselves. They couldn't go to work, being so tired and traumatised. I felt so sorry for them. I know that I'll never forget what I saw and heard there at that house as long as I live. I would not like to go through that horror again, myself, ever!

Chapter Four

Annunciation

The strange events at the Fahey's home received almost worldwide attention in 1997. Most newspapers in England and Ireland and some in Mainland Europe carried reports, as did TV stations. This, however, is the first book, commissioned by the Fahey family, and a film is expected to follow.

While the strange events at the Fahey's home were ongoing for eight month, October of May 1997, it was only in May that the haunting came to a head, in intensity and terror. It was then that serious media coverage began, circa May 8th to 9th.

The local newspapers City Tribune of May 9th read ;

Jackie Fahey said that some months ago the family [only] began to notice a foul smell, like that of urine or rotten meat. But it was only later that the disturbances increased in fury, with pictures flying, vases smashing, etc.

Mike Fahey said that it appeared that some spirit was trying to protect his eight month old niece. Sometimes the door to her room would be hold shut against them. Jackie resumes; "Sandra Ramdhanie told us that the spirit was jealous of baby Sarah and wanted the love and attention that she was getting of her mum and the family. That's why it was throwing things around, basically it was throwing a typical tantrum." Fr. Colum Kilcoyne, in his column in the same paper cites exorcist Fr. Sean Conaty on the Late Late Show [Irelands long running talk show 50yrs and still going strong] Fr. Conaty has a test for establishing the existence of evil spirits; He brings holy water into the room. The evil spirit goes wild. He goes out and changes to plain water, and this has no effect at all. Seemingly the evil has more respect for holy water than many of us today.

Reporter, Aidan Sheehan of the Evening Herald [Dublin] sat up on Thursday night, May 8th, and witnessed noises and the "spontaneous combustion" of the life size heavy porcelain dog on the hearth. Brain Mc Donald of the Irish—Independent carries the story and a picture of Fr. Malachi Hallinan leaving the house on Wednesday evening, May 7th after celebrating Mass at the Fahey's home.

The Daily Mirror had an account on Saturday, May 10th, and again on May 13th about the healing ceremony.

In the Connacht Tribune, May 16th Martha Fahey, mother of baby Sarah says:

The disturbances started when drilling and extension work began next door, eight months ago. This was also when Sarah arrived home. Sandra Ramdhanie came on Sunday last and conducted a healing ceremony. She put me sitting in the centre of a circle of friends and family members, acting as and imagining that I was holding the spirit-baby gently and lovingly in my arms. Thus did the spirit gain its freedom and left peacefully, "smiling happy."

The Sun newspaper of May 14th deals with; (A) the house mass; and (b) the healing ceremony (the partial one on the Saturday 11th).

'(A), During the Mass the baby spirit upstairs began to cry. The priest raised his voice, as did the spirit, and the priest again, until finally he was almost shouting. He was shaking with fear. Afterwards the haunting only got worse.'

The Connacht Sentinel of Tuesday, May 14th dealt with the healing ceremony:

Mike Fahey was one of those present and part of the human circle in baby's room. Sandra used tele-kinesis to contact the spirit. All of those present saw the soul of the ghost-baby lift from the room through a tunnel of light. The baby was smiling and was dressed in white and glowing in a white light.

In a Sunday Tribune article Mike (Fahey) says that it felt like there were two presences in the house: a baby, and adult who is either threatening Sarah or trying to protect her.

The Sunday Independent of May 18th has a full article on Sandra Ramdhaine. Her father knew Brendan Behan, and by all accounts was quite a character himself. She says that she believes in the holistic approach to healing;

'I usually get the people that doctors, priests and psychiatrists cannot help. I prescribe fun, happiness and love. I don't believe in evil spirits, therefore I am never afraid. Spirits just need love, like us just being available to "listen" helps spirits, just like it helps someone with, say, depression. Listen and love, that's it".

The Star newspaper on May 26th, described the healing ritual; 'Sandra healed the spirit in a cleansing ceremony using Tibetan incense, stone crystals, affirmations and herbs, while family members held hands in a ring while visualising the spirit-baby rising in golden light to heaven.'

The Sun May 26th, mention the TV documentary for L.W.T series Strange but true, narrated by Michael Aspel, featuring the Fahey family haunting. The Mirror, June 14th 1998, deal with a proposed Hollywood film of the haunting. The August 22nd edition continues with the news that Hollywood director Ron Howard is being touted for the job, with perhaps Sandra writing the screenplay. Howard directs the TV serial Far and Way.

The Sunday World September 28th, 1997, reports that psychic Sandra has been visited by the spirit of the late Princess Diana. Sandra says that Diana was pregnant at the time of her death and was about to convert to Islam. Her spirit is still disturbed and remains at the scene of the car cash in Paris tunnel.

Diana "says" that her driver had simply been blinded by the headlights of an on-coming car. There was no sinister conspiracy. Diana didn't want to die, she too was a healer.

The News of the World, February 14th, 1999, describes Sandra's techniques:

She relies on gentle persuasion to get the ghost to move on to a better place. She "chats" with the spirit to convince it that it would be happier elsewhere. Many spirits are being roused by the modern upsurge in building, demolition and renovation. These spirits are trapped between here and the after-life, usually because they were deeply depressed or had died violently. "I meditate and communicate with them through telepathy and advise them to move on to the next life to their loved ones. Spirits can lie dormant for years but excavation work disturbs them because it interferes with earth's energies. There is no need to be afraid. Everyone has psychic powers, but some are more telepathic than others, and have developed those powers."

The Galway People March 15th,1999. Eggshells were found on two consecutive days on the floor of Mikes bedroom. Real shells, but how did they get there, doors and windows were closed and locked when they were away?!!

When put into a container the shells actually grow in size and in volume. The scene was reminiscent of a birth or a hatching of a new life, as if the spirit-baby had been born again.

In folklore too it is said that if someone wanted to curse his neighbours land he would bury an egg or spread egg-shells about. Was there a malign influence about? It is more likely here that it signified birth. Or could it have indicated the death/ destruction of a foetus? So perhaps the shells were communicating a message? In the R.T.E. Guide, Sandra describes herself as a healer, psychic and psychic researcher—a sort of psychic agony aunt. She is not a fortune-teller or a spiritualist, believing that there is no needed to know about the future or the after-life. It is unfair to call on spirits that have passed over, she says. She is opposed to gimmickry, spoon-bending tricks, etc. Why not heal and cure instead? Many of her clients for counselling,etc. Are in Hollywood, California.

'A spirit may be attached to a house, etc. through fondness, or because of depression or a violent death. She doesn't "exercise" or banish a ghost, believing that it is cruel to an already disturbed spirit. Rather she communicates kindly and gently and helps them move over. All spirits want to pass over to the afterlife. Her services are called for mostly in Cork, Kerry and Wicklow a d at Halloween and May Day as in the Fahey's case'.

In the Irish Tatler, Sandra says that she prefers to "re-house" spirits, rather that "evict" them as exorcists do. They were once human beings on this earth and deserve to be treated kindly, rather than with fear and ignorance. She has never encountered an "evil" spirit and knows of no one injured by a ghost. She has helped the F.B.I. in detective cases and has solved murders. The Catholic Church, however, recognises evil spirits, most notably of all—Satan, and so tends to banish or exorcise spirits. She, however, prefers to show love and healing towards the trouble soul, and to gently coax them "over". In her own book; trapped between two worlds. Sandra defines ghosts and poltergeist, etc, as spirits so trapped. Due to hurt, pain, sadness, wrong, anger or vengeance, these spirits are frozen in space ands time and are either unable or unwilling to move on to the afterlife. She relates a story remarkably similar to the Fahey's experience. It was a haunted house in Dublin. She discovered the spirit to be a sad, gaunt woman of about 55, who had lived in a house on the same site at the turn of the century. She was the only daughter of a well to do family, as a young lady she had been seduced by her uncle and she borne a child. The family got rid of the baby and confined the young woman to a private room. She lived as a recluse for the rest of her life and finally hanged herself when in her 50's. Most spirits are poltergeists, not ghosts, Sandra says; The latter do not display the active intelligence of poltergeists, and seem locked into a sad replay of some traumatic or significant event, mechanically going through the motions. Both she and the clairvoyant agree that the motive in the Fahey's case was a poltergeist.

Just as in the Fahey's case, Sandra has investigated many a baby incidents; A lady called Mary recounted going into her baby son's room to find him jumping up and down in a sitting position in his cot, as though being bounced by invisible hands. He was engrossed and laughing happily, with his toys floating in the air around him.

Chapter Five

Exposition

Photographic Phenomena

During the disturbance at the Fahey's home in May 1997 a keen photographer, Andrew Kavanagh, arrived. He pictured in the first photo there. {See colour section}. Note there is a green light emanating downwards from the lampshade, but not upwards through the opening on the top? And the room is painted in magnolia colour with no green at all! Also the light is not diffusing all over the room, or even out to the angle of the shade, but is shining downwards directly. Remember too that baby Sarah always pointed to the man in the bulb or the baby in the bulb. And the power that exploded the ceramic dog in the front room below travelled all along the TV aerial which terminated beside the dog, and was burned. So, does a supernatural power/energy utilise domestic power as a mode of conveyance? But most dramatically of all here, the light was not on as Andrew was filming in darkness, virtually! This is the baby's room

Jonathan Fahey

Investigation of 11th of May, 1997 (Saturday)

Location; 286, Corrib Park, Galway City.
Category; Poltergeist
By Andrew Kavangh

Having arrived in Galway and taken the precaution Of finding a hostel to leave the gar in, I rang Jackie Fahey at 9.45 p.m. He sounded weary on the phone, and I felt that my intrusion would be one too many after the week they'd had, but none the less he agreed to see me at 10.30 p.m. The taxi-man who took me to Corrib Park, like most people in this town at the moment, was well acquainted with the story. I told him I had come as an impartial observer, with the intention only of spending the night in the slightest activity on video. The taxi-man's seanchai warning about spirits did nothing for my nerves, though. Having arrived armed with my logic, I was quivering with apprehension at the end of this short car journey. (Seachai-Old Gaelic for storyteller) On arrival, I met Jackie and he's wife Esther and their son Mike and daughter Martha. They had that patina of fear and exhaustion about them that one associates with the traumatised and truly afraid. There were others in the house, including the psychic Sandra Rhandhamie, who had just performed a healing in one of the affected rooms.

I talked to them about the activity, and was surprised to hear that Martha and her daughter, Sarah Louise (whom the disturbances are believed to be focused on), were not on the night of the heaviest activity, the previous Thursday. I had believed that a latent psychic ability in one or either may have been the cause of objects (or even shattering, as had been seen).

Cry From Beyond

Having removed the psychic possibility, I suggest that perhaps Radon gases, which occur in under suburban Galway with more regularity than any other part of Europe, may be building up under the house. Of course, I'd have to check my science on this one, but I offer to contact an expert on radiation to come and test the place out. The Fahey's asked me where crying voices and door handles turning fit with that theory and I am forced to think again.

My only course of action is to stay in the room and try to document a paranormal occurrence. Having come to Galway with my theory and logic, I now feeling decidedly regretful of my gung ho attitude. I have to acknowledge that there may be a spirit here and I must respect that. The Fahey's all seem genuine and I have no cause doubt them. These people have no airs or graces and certainly do not strike one as actors. The hoax theory doesn't really apply.

Jackie shows me to Sarah Louise's room and I begin to set up. He looks edgy and very keen to get back downstairs, we don't talk long, as I set up my gear, I'm conscious for the first time of the auspiciousness of this occasion. My imagination starts to ramble as I go over in my mind the events that have taken place here in the last weeks. I knoe that I have to nip these fears in the bud, it's going to be along night. I've been here all of fifteen minutes and nothing seems out of place or weird yet. I've heard the odd click and rumble but nothing that you'd not hear in any other house and ignore as normal everyday noises of a neighbour hood that has thin walls. I am a bit scared, but the one thing that I have to my advantage is that I've been through this before and will probably been to scared to run away if anything happens anyway. This is a personal challenge. None of the other members of the household will even venture upstairs now, and I am alone in the haunted room for the night, if I can stick it out. The opportunity to catch something truly extraordinary on film heartens me, and I realise that I am in a unique and fortuitous position.

12.55 a.m.;

We are fast approaching the hour when it is all supposed to happen. It comforts me to think if this is a ghost, it's a child, and I don't feel any fear of him/her. Only my own apprehension in the face of what might be a unique and fascinating experience. The camera is running, trained on the child's dresses, which seem to be a favourite mover. I also have my stills camera ready, Dictaphone for verbal comments, and this notebook. An audio cassette is also running.

01.15 a.m.;

Jackie comes up to check on me and his breathing is very shaky. This is the time for whatever it is to show up. He tells me that the room is usually ice-cold by now and that is a signal for something to happen. There is a bit of nip, but it's just a draughter, I'm sure. This room is a lot warmer than my one in Dublin.

01.20 a.m.;

The audio cassette that Mike left running reached its length and stopped, making one of those electrical pop noises. I nearly jumped out of my skin.

01.25a.m.;

An upstairs door handle rattles. There's no-one upstairs apart from me.

01.28 a.m.;

Another caller tries to get in to see the place. That's four since I arrived at 10.30p.m. God only knows what it must be like during the day.

01.35 a.m.

Mike Fahey phone the Gardai (police) to report two cars watching the house from across the road.

01.40 a.m.;

A biscuit break downstairs and this is brought to my attention. The smallest occurrences seem to disproportnate in a time such as this. I am feeling cold spots every now and again in the room.

01.47 a.m.;

Police arrive to see off the stalkers. Very prompt. I hear a baby crying but I'm sure it must be next door. I'll check to see if there are any babies next door tomorrow.

01.55 a.m.;

The house has now gone quite, so I assume that everyone has turned in for the night. I am feeling a bit tired myself, but am still very alert.

02.05 a.m.;

Starting the third run on the camcorder, I take a self portrait photograph "investigating". I've been here three and half hours now, and time has flown, quite the contrary to what I had expected.

2.10 a.m.;

Weird breathing noises on the landing. The door is open and I am staring right at it. I tell myself it is snoring from downstairs.

2.20 a.m.;

Auto focus on camera is trying to focus on something, but there is nothing there that is visible to me. But does the camera "see" something?

2.45 a.m.;

A man arrives asking if he can stop by tomorrow sometime for a look around. Mike is calm and tolerant. As for me, the sound of the doorbell nearly finished me off.

2.50 a.m.;

Mike tells me that the caller was only someone from next door checking on them.

3.00 a.m.;

I start the fourth run on the camcorder and go downstairs. The neighbours have arrived and Jackie eventually goes with them. I stay up with Mike, and he tells me about the "exorcism", and about Sandra and about the "Bishop" Michael Cox's involvement in the case.

4.30 a.m.;

I start the fifth run on the camcorder. I will check these tapes for disturbances on my return to Dublin. Mike tells me that there are no babies next door (Cr 01.45 a.m.) and that no-one was asleep (CR 02.10 a.m.) when I heard the weird breathing noises.

5.30 a.m.;

Mike shows me the fragments of the shattered jug and the porcelain dog, which they were going to throw out. I suggest Kirlian photography of the fragments. He shoes me a crucifix they had been given which was used in an exorcism. I photograph these, and a mirror, which was also disturbed by the phenomena.

6.15 a.m.;

It is daylight and raining heavily, and I packed up my gear t head back to Eyre Square. I promise to come back tomorrow.

12th of May 1997, 1.00p.m. (Sunday):

I arrive back at Corrib Park and chat to the family and amongst others, Sandra, the journalist Molly Mc Annually-Bourke and Declan White. I go through some of the footage on view-finder of the camcorder, but nothing appears to nothing appears to have moved in the room. I will develop my stills when I get home to see if I caught anything there.

As I leave at 3 o' clock, Sandra is doing another 'healing' and the Strange but True TV people are arriving. There is a positive feeling in the house, and although I am mentally tired. I leave feeling charged and exuberant. I have a tangible that whatever was haunting the Fahey's family of Corrib Park has been put to rest.

Interesting here that Andrew Kavanagh heard a baby's crying and breathing sounds, and that his camera automatically focussed on something. And this was after Sandra had already performed a partial healing, on that same day, May 11th, 1997. What might he have witnessed

If he had been there before Sandra, and if Sarah-Louise had been in the bedroom to possibly "invite" the spirit-baby to appear. And who turned the door-knob?

Remarkable too that Andrew comments on Martha's and Sarah-Louise's absence on the previous Thursday night, May 9th, when the disturbance was at its most severe. How perceptive that he suggests, like the psychic and clairvoyant, that either Martha or Sarah may have been the cause of the events. But couldn't one of the other's latent psychic ability have operated also by remote control from a distance? (as it apparently did in the drummer boy story in this book).

It likely, however, that Andrew did miss out on possible photographic evidence due to Sandra's prior arrival. What dramatic pictures we may have witnessed otherwise. Still, the peculiar shades and hues and light patterns captured are interesting phenomena, nevertheless. Significantly, he states that it is only the Fahey's photographs from that roll of film which have he greenish hue, even though many more of them were taken with flash. This means that the camera and the film were not faulty. Andrew cannot account for the difference. Also, he says, that the white dove-shaped light (flash reflection?) does not appear on the other flash photographs, and anyway he stands to the side so that no reflection will occur.

Chapter Six

Reconciliation

Sandra Ramdhanie Healer

The Fahey family owe their deliverance and their sanity to this very special women. Sandra is a beautiful soul. Her warmth, kindness and love is tangible, in her presence, some say she has a glow about her.

Not at all the image one has of a psychic. One would expect an austere, severe and cold person, someone conversant with evil as well as good. But Sandra don't believe in evil at all. Perhaps that is why she is fearless in the face of the supernatural.

She is a mixture of all religions and none, her family background is of Hindu and Presbyterian faiths. She feels that she is a reincarnation of a Chinese Doctor, so she may have traces of Zen and Confucius in her psyche too—she uses Tibetan incense. She is therefore blissfully free of all religious phobias, fears, superstitions, hang-ups and scruples. She is a priestess of Isis and practise good only. She does not countenance Satan or evil practices of devil worship or animal torture or sacrifice. She does not support destruction of trees and the environment and fox-hunting and coursing like many Christians do. Yet the Catholic Church might look askance at her. What then ought she think of them? Our Lord said of those who would judge others. 'You see a tiny splinter of wood in your neighbours eye, yet fail to notice the log/ beam in your own'. But probably most telling of all; 'Can a devil perform good works?' By their fruit's . . . . ? Sandra performs good works only—ask the Fahey's. Why then might some Catholics criticise her? Sandra has healed on a Sundays, as the Lord did on the Sabbath. And He was criticised by the clergy of His day— the Scribes and Pharisees!

God is love, and love is the manifestation of God. Loved healed this haunting. Who channelled that love? The Catholic Church believes it is the one true Church. But God's healing love in this case was evidently mediated through another channel, a non-Catholic, perhaps even a non-Christian! Does this suggest then that the Roman Catholic Church is not the exclusive repository of Divine love, wisdom, healing and truth?

Christ gave an example of this paradox in His parable; "The Good Samaritan". When He asked; "who is my neighbour", He went outside the 'one, true, orthodox Jewish line, to the outcast Samaritans, Because it was a Samaritan who showed love. A possible proof too that one is not "saved" or justified by faith alone, but by love and good works as well. Sandra was the good Samaritan in this case, yet she is not of the "orthodox" faith! Ironically she had to heal a situation that was caused by the one true Church ethos, possibly. In what other Church might a member feel compelled to kill in order to uphold the moral code of it's Church? And notwithstanding that one of that Church Commandments says; Thou Shalt not kill?

Where's that spirit-baby now? Those at the healing ceremony saw him/her move on, smiling. Is he/she gone back to limbo—if he/she was there? Is he/she gone to heave? Do babies go to heaven? Is Sarah-Louise he/she re-incarnation? If not, is he/she now waiting for a suitable vacancy to recur in some other family? Is this just a flash back-or is it real? If Martha and baby had left the home at the beginning, would the haunting have ceased? Are unmarried girls as mother's a convenient vehicle for the re-incarnation of babies waiting in "Limbo"?

If Sandra is correct then the spirit baby has moved on. And if reincarnation does occur, then that spirit has found another human home, or will do in the future.

But who exactly then is Sarah-Louise? Sandra says she is not a reincarnation, and a clairvoyant engaged for a second opinion agrees. They say Sarah is just herself, a normal, happy, clever child. Yet she does not resemble her parents or family in anyway at all? The clairvoyant says that it is Martha who was at the centre of the story, and not Sarah-Louise. But he says that Martha is not a reincarnation either.

Chapter Seven

Rationalisation

What precisely was the cause of the haunting at the Fahey's home in 1996/97?

It is generally agreed that such occurrences have a source, a prime-mover. In this case it does seem that the cause was a killing years before, and the effect was the haunting here.

Why didn't the spirit of the murdered baby move to the afterlife immediately? Why was it apparently dormant for 90 odd years? Why didn't it become an angle in heaven, as many Catholic's believe? Perhaps it did move on to limbo, and waited there in the twilight zone until a suitable foster family emerged. This writer hear is a Catholic, but the views expressed here are not orthodox, according to Catholic priest friend; The Catholic Church says that reincarnation is

Not a precept of Roman Catholic Church doctrine, indeed it is a heresy.

Lucky then that the one true holy Catholic Church does not any longer burn dissenters at the stake—what a strange manifestation of the Christian love that was! But then it was also once a heresy to demonstrate that the earth is round and that the sun is the centre of our universe!

Sandra gives her views elsewhere here as to why the soul of the spirit-baby didn't initially move on to the next life, she believes that it was trapped between the two worlds. But how and why?

The Roman Catholic Church taught that illegitimate, stillborn,

Aborted babies went to Limbo, forever. Limbo was a state of greyness, of half-life, not unlike the classical portrayal of Hades, it seems.

Now, one can believe in Limbo, but not as a permanent eternal state. Why should innocent babies be punished to half-life forever? This is a logical fallacy, if God's love is infinite and just? It is believable that babies sleep-wait in Limbo until a suitable vacancy occurs in a surrogate family and they are reawakened to a new earth life. They cannot go to heaven as babies because they are too immature to know God or to have made a choice in will and full knowledge and reason for or against God. We have to earn the right to enter heaven?

And human babies cannot become angels? Angels are a different species, pure spirits only, and not born of woman. Human babies possess both body and spirit, corporally.

But why is it, apparently, that only babies who suffer a violent deaths haunt people and places? Or is it just that natural death babies are not disturbed and haunt us benignly and unnoticed? It would seem that Limbo is a sort of twilight zone, half-way between heaven and earth, and is visible or sensible to us in extreme cases. I believe that it is the Divine plan for all humans to first live on earth, and to at least reach the age of reason and full knowledge, before entering heaven. A baby has not yet decided for God, or earned the right to heaven through a life of trails and suffering's?

I believe that God allows every human being a chance to live to maturity in this life, and therefore, reincarnation is necessary for these who die young. Little Jamie Bolger (2 yrs) was brutally murdered in Bootle, Liverpool. His parents had a new baby a year later, and they say that he is uncannily like Jamie in every way. I believe that he is Jamie, and that if his parents hadn't had any more children after Jamie, that he would have come back later in some other suitable family. Which may be why some people say; I have lived before. He would have waited in Limbo, and is now born again into his own family? Perhaps God selects the most suitable and compatible family for such babies, so that some babies may have to wait longer for a suitable vacancy Limbo must be that temporary waiting room.

Is Sarah Louise Fahey then a reincarnation of the spirit baby? Sandra doesn't think so. But this writer does, and the Fahey family do. And for a number of reasons;

The family say that she is different in every way, looks, personality, intelligence,independence. They feel that she is not one of them. She does not look like her parents, or behave like them. She is very independent and acts alone. She is highly intelligent and has an authorities air and strong willed. And although she is three years old she is wise beyond her years, more like a six or twelve year old, She doesn't seem as innocent as other three year olds. One feels about her that "she knows something". Perhaps when she's a teenager she will recall a previous existence? Or she may forget everything.

If Sarah-Louise is a re-incarnation, perhaps it happened in 1996 because a "suitable vacancy" arose. The location of the house was exactly the same, although the family background is entirely different. The opportunity was certainly there however. Martha Fahey was pregnant in 1996 but wasn't married, or established in regular nuclear union of husband and wife. It was an opportunity for the spirit-baby to be "adopted" by her in the form of Sarah-Louise, a sort of "foster-child". But Martha felt no empathy with the spirit-baby at all? Then again Sarah-Louise could be a reincarnation of someone else still. Or she may be just "herself" after all!

A major flaw in this theory in this case, however, is the time delay. Why the gap of 90 years, since the 1900? Surely a "suitable vacancy" would have occurred almost immediately, in 1906, somewhere in the world—even in Galway? The Fahey's didn't live in the house when their own two children were born. Perhaps Sandra is right. She says that Sarah-Louise is not the other baby. They played together—as separate beings, she says.

Sandra believes that it was the disruption caused by building work next door, that disturbed the spirit-baby, or the arrival of a new baby that re-awakened it. But if building had never occurred, how long would the spirit-baby have slumbered on, in Limbo or the twilight zone or wherever? This doesn't seem a very "concrete" theory! How can walls restrain a spirit?

Now perhaps babies do go to heaven or even become angles, and that baby may have passed on immediately in the 1900's. The haunting then may just be a vivid "play-back" of a past event, like a "memory". Sandra believes that because of the violent and unhappy nature of his/

she death that the spirit-baby did not, could not or would not pass on and remained "trapped between our world and the other side".

But this is not logical to me. Either all babies go to heaven or none do. Why should violence alter the divine or natural order of things? If a baby is going to enjoy eternal bliss in heaven why should (s) he delay going there—for any reason, even violence. Once in heaven all would be forgotten-even murder! Therefore, it would seem to me that babies do not go to heaven: that it is God's plan that we come to him through maturity, suffering, testing and free will in this earthly life first, only. There is no plan B, no other way, or little angles option.

Why should violence trap a soul here below? Our Lord suffered a violent, brutal death. Martyr's, like St. Stephen saw heaven open to receive his soul and commended his spirit of God—as indeed Christ Himself had done at His death on the cross. All violent deaths! But all were mature adults!

Yet haunting by mature adults do occur. And they do seem to be usually connected with violent demise. Why don't these spirits pass on? They don't need to be reincarnated, presumably, since they have already lived almost a full life? The explanation may be beyond human comprehension or may be one of two reasons:

(1) A soul cannot move on until a wrong has been righted or avenged; or

(2) The soul has moved on at death, but its violent death still sends shocks pulses of energy down the airwaves of time like a video/audio playback or recording, or flashback, or memory, or reply, or reverberation.

Of (1) above I can't understand why a soul would be trapped here just because of a violent death. It must be because that soul cannot forgive the wrong-doer, and so can't enter heaven until it forgives. It may want revenge first. But why not leave revenge/ justice to God and move on to far happier existence than this twilight zone. Or perhaps some wronged souls are evil themselves and don't want to move on to heaven anyway; or just may be too disturbed to let go and move on.

Of (2) above it is plausible that shock waves could reverberate long after the violent death and departure of the soul to the next life, in a sort of surreal or reflective playback of a real event long past. But is the spirit present or not In the subsequent haunting?

[N.B.] Christian/ Catholic terminology is employed here because it is that most familiars to this writer, and to most readers. Of course the events of this story may have a non-Christian rationale to other readers. Views expressed here are mere personal opinions only.]

Limbo

Even though Roman Catholics were taught about Limbo at school, and it was described in the catechism, the Church no longer recognises such a state. Limbo was an invention of St. Augustine in order to explain what happens to unbaptised babies who die. It never became an official doctrine of R.C.C however, despite being included in the catechism.

Chapter Eight

Re-Incarnation

Many Eastern religions believe in reincarnation. The R.C.C. does not. But many, many people including Catholics, have testified to a previous life(s), with demonstrable and verifiable particulars. Most of these cases concern babies and children, almost invariably involving death in a first life. We occasionally hear of wise babies, mature beyond their years, we get the feeling that they know something. That is certainly the case with little Sarah-Louise Fahey!

Jenny Randle's and Peter Hough in their book life after death and the world beyond cite a number of interesting cases;

Juliet from a small Lancashire town, remembers an incident in her bedroom when she was only a few months old. Strange lights came to play with her? Not unlike our story hear.

Nicola Peart from Keighley in Yorkshire, at two years old asked her present mother why she was a boy last time, when her mum was a Mrs. Benson, living in Haworth, a few miles away. An examination of the surprising story revealed that the child had been killed on the railway line by a steam engine. When the Peart's visited Haworth, Nicola pointed out the stone-house in which she had lived.

Investigations revealed that her amazing account was indeed true. The Benson's had lived there. Their son, born in 1875, had died as a small child. Nicola was recalling her past life of 100 years earlier. She is not alone. Children, often between the ages of about three and eight, come up with such spontaneous stories quite frequently.

The distinguished psychiatrist Dr. Ian Stephenson of the University of Virginia, The U.S.A. has compiled such case histories, mostly of children, from all over the world.

Ravi Shankar, the eminent musician, was born in the Uttar Pradesh region of India in 1951. When he was two he told his parents that in a previous life he had been murdered as a boy, and less than a mile away from his present home. He later even named the two killers. Professor Stevenson established that the account was true, and had occurred just six months before Ravi's (re)birth. Ravi's evidence was not accepted as legal proof against his killers, however,

It would seem, in this case, that Ravi didn't return just for vengeance. Apparently he was merely given his human right to live a full natural life here below. And he was / is not a Christian. So God, then cares for all of his children regardless of religious denomination, it would seem? Noteworthy too that in most cases the reincarnations occur close to the original districts. In the Fahey's case it is virtually in the same spot, that is if it is a case of reincarnation.

Randle and Hough continue with the case researched by Californian Psychotherapist Hemendra Banerjee;

Cry From Beyond

In 1980, three year old Romy Cree's started to talk to her parents in Des Moines, Iowa, about her recent life as a 37 year old man, killed in a motorcycle accident. Another case was of a 52 year old man. [so, even adults, it seems get a chance to live again, though of a mature age? Perhaps this is because they hadn't know God first time round]

Stevenson knew of two British cases in which children were re-born again into their own families. Most of his cases showed reincarnation to have occurred near to the original home area.

Proof that these children weren't just tuning in to general psychic experiences, is the fact that they always claim the images to be from their own past lives, and in one case only. And this, despite the apparent suitability of the children's minds as channels of communication for outsiders as well. Significantly, none of the cases studied mention an afterlife or a heaven. This surely suggests that those who were reborn had not been to heaven in the meantime, or to Purgatory? The meantime period is apparently blank to the memory. So it would seem that the soul had waited in a slumber-like, half-life state—or perhaps the Limbo of the Christian belief.

But what then of case of Deirdre in the Randle's and Hough book? Her newborn baby died, and Deirdre pined for her for months. One night at the infant's grave, she felt herself being pulled into a tunnel of light. She found herself sitting on a hill watching some adults playing with a children. She instinctively knew that one of the children was her baby.

What was this a vision of Deidre's then. Was it heaven, or of Limbo? Was the baby now living happily and permanently in the next life, or was she waiting there temporarily before being reincarnated?

There may be a suggestion here that it is only cases of violent deaths that are granted reincarnation? But again, can a baby see god and heaven without first having gotten to know god in an earthly life? And if so, then what is the purpose of an earthly existence at all then? Reason, therefore, suggests that a mature earthly life is pre-requisite to eternal life, and the only means thereto. Consider another case in the Randle's book; Ellen had a near-death experience (NDE) while undergoing an op in1994. She founded herself in a garden, and a three year old girl has taken her hand. The child resembled my own daughter who miscarried three years before. This then was my own grand-child. Also there, excited, hopping and skipping, is a little boy of about six or seven years of age dressed in ordinary earthly clothes. He was also a miscarried child, of a family friend, I knew intuitively. Now, he said, he had chosen me as his grandmother too and would return to me on earth in two years time.

Ellen was asked was this heaven? Her answer was unexpected;

The garden is wondrous and beautiful, but it is just a meeting place. The spirits go back to somewhere else, they didn't say where. They do not live in this garden.

Perhaps this answers the earlier question; are these spirit-babies in heaven? Ellen's answer suggest no—just a meeting place. Where they are seems to be mysterious and unexplained. Could they then be I Limbo, waiting? It would seem then that babies, no matter how they die, do not go to heaven. And it would seem that they must be reincarnated! Does this suggest that only adults—or those who have attained the age of reason-can go to heaven?

Perhaps one has to earn the right to enter heaven, and to decide by an act of will to choose good rather than evil. Babies cannot do this.

So then, reincarnation does seem to be a real and true phenomenon, despite the R.C.C. pronouncements. But the Church's claims for a Limbo would appear to be accurate. Limbo, however, is not a place of eternal or permanent banishment. Rather it is a state of slumber, of half-life, of waiting a state of temporary sojourn.

Sarah-Louise Fahey is now four years old (2000 A.D) She is cute, pretty intelligent and vivacious; and fiercely independent, even of her mother, Martha.

She is more attached to her grand-father Jackie. Jackie feels that she is not like one of us. Her looks, mannerisms, attitudes, etc, are totally different. He believes that Sarah-Louise knows that she is different. She is a wise baby, clever and mature beyond her years. She gives the impression that she knows something more.!

Jackie has tried gently to find out what she does know, but he finds her evasive. She talks about the baby in the bulb coming to play with her and her toys. He's asked her if she has lived before in a previous life. She slowly answers yeah, in the bulb? And she said that she died!? Jackie is not sure if she really understands and means what she says. He suspects that she does understand but finds it uncomfortable to talk about it, so he doesn't like to probe too much, but she does seem to equate herself with the baby in the bulb.

So, is Sarah a reincarnation of the murdered baby? Psychic Sandra doesn't believe so. Neither does the clairvoyant. Therefore we ought to bow to the opinion of the experts. Perhaps as she grows up Sarah will recall or reveal more, or maybe that memory will gradually fade away.

She may find the whole thing hurtful and try to suppress it. Maybe we will never know the full story, but the Fahey's believe that there is something there.

Logically it would seem that Sandra is right. If Sarah were the reincarnation of the baby-spirit who died, then how could that same spirit-baby exit the house in a beam of light at the healing ceremony, leaving Sarah crying at its departure? This definitely suggests two discrete and separate individuals.

Perhaps Sarah may be another spirit-baby altogether, who got in ahead of the murdered one? Perhaps the latter resented this and therefore caused all of the trouble at the Fahey's the house. This, however, is very unlikely, and rather fanciful, but the Fahey's were aware of an adult presence there as well, which was more threatening and sinister. Could this be the killer of the baby?

The family felt it to be a physically strong, male presence, e.g. in the throwing of vases, etc, and the sinister foot-tapping at the phone. Yet Sandra saw only the baby-spirit in the house? And Sarah is not a reincarnation she insists. A mystery unresolved, indeed! In her book, Sandra relates a poltergeist case involving vase-throwing,etc, and she saw that spirit to be a baby or child. So physical force doesn't necessarily imply a strong manly presence then. Will-power is the key.

Other poltergeist phenomena common to such cases are noises, movements, footsteps, doors opening or closing, lights going on and off, items being flung or smashed, and with spirit presence being invisible. So the haunting in the Fahey's

Case was a poltergeist spirit, exercising psycho-kinetic energy, by remote-control, it would seem?, but who was the prime-mover or cause?

Yet, there was a ghost appearance also. Mike Fahey saw a brief, once off glimpse of a girl about 12 in a white frilly dress in the hallway of their home. Jackie says that his sister died at that age, at the time of her Confirmation? And Sarah said that here was a strange man standing in the doorway of her bedroom?

Further positive evidence of reincarnation in general was in an RTE TV documentary on a Co. Donegal family whose six year old daughter disappeared while wandering in moor-land in 1980. Today, that child's twin sister has a daughter of about six who described as the image of the missing child, in looks, mannerisms, etc.

There is then, apparently, sufficient proof of actual reincarnation, especially of children under the age of reason, knowledge and exercise of free will. This should not shock, but rather testify to the infinite-wisdom, justice and love of God, the creator, a God who generously gives a second chance.

A distinguished patriotic Irish lady at the turn of the century had a child following a temporary affair in France. The child died in infancy. Later, and now married (to another man) she had another child, a boy. In a biography of her life she relates with maternal intuition and absolute certainly that this boy was reincarnation of her first child, and identical in every way, and resembling more the original father. This boy grew up to be one the world's most famous and respected public figures, in law and politics.

Therefore, it must happen that many families have a cuckoo in their nest, I.e., a child not directly their own, or at least from a different time.

Abundant evidence it would seem that reincarnation is indeed a reality, but why should we (or some churches) be disturbed by this? Does it not show that each soul is precious, undying and eternal, and that premature physical death does not destroy the soul/ spirit. It goes marching on, forever, retaining its original unique personality, even in a second, separate family. A sort of cuckoo child as it were. A cuckoo chick is fostered out to parents of another species, but it is always a cuckoo. Is it not more beautiful still that God gives a child a second chance to live on this earth, albeit in a surrogate family. Evidence surely of a just, loving and caring Deity. Amen.

Ancient Influence?
(The "Lye" of the land)

The psychic said that she "felt" strong vibration of ancient "leys" in the surrounding distrait of the Fahey's home. Psychic forces are channelled along these "leys" or physical courses such a streams or rivers or pathways. This is not to claim that ancient influences had any bearing on the Fahey's case.

The following extracts from the "Archaeological Inventory of Co. Galway" by Paul Gosling, and Taylor and Skinner's map of 1778, give an outline of the lie of the land in times past. The places cited are in the immediate vicinity of the Fahey's home, on the north side of Galway city and close to the great waterway of the River Corrib, the course of human concentration and commerce for thousands of years.

Artificial channels

Sarah-Louise repeatedly spoke of the baby in the light bulb. The porcelain dog in the Fahey's sitting room was smashed by a power which ran along a TV aerial cable beside it, apparently.

It would seem then that modern electrical cables and accessories are utilised as channels of the supernatural. The two accounts from the magazine Ireland's Own-n here are not dissimilar to our own story, especially that of the "voice in the Candle Flame", coincidentally about a Fahey also!?

From-

"Archaeological Inventory of Co. Galway"

Castle—(site of)

Opposite Terry land Castle at fording point. In1574 owned by Martin Lynch, Esq. Described in Down Survey (Stratford) 1657 as a castle and a thatched cabin within a bawn or stone wall. Brewery built on site c. 1800. Fragments of a stout wall (bawn?) and ivy-covered dove-cot, (circular angle tower in U.C.G. grounds).

Ring fort (hachured)

In rough grazing and scrub land overlooking River Corrib. Circular cashel of collapsed dry-stone wall, overlain by modern field wall at west side. Inside is a D—shape stone hut.

Church (Site of)

St. James Chapel, on bank of the Corrib. Erected in 1509 by the Lynch's Demolished 1920's.

Holy well;

50 metres to the south of the church site. Destroyed in construction of mill-race.

Stream

Shruffaun-a-caislaun. Near Westside road of today and Corrib Park Estate.

Tower;

At Shantalla.

Note; Taylor& Skinner Roads of Ireland map 1778. At Galway City north, see castle ruins opposite Terry land on west bank of the Corrib river, thus "Newcastle" perhaps Corrib Park Housing estate nearby. [map with photo's enclosed]

Chapter Nine

Revesraries

Phantom large black dogs are a common phenomenon of reported ghostly experiences, worldwide. During the haunting at this house, Jackie had a most disturbing nightmare. He doesn't know, however, if it has any relevance to his home.

He dreamt of seeing a large, manor-type house, with a stone or castellated façade. There was a limestone plaque on the wall at the entrance with a crest or coat-of-arms embossed thereon [see colour plate]. Then suddenly two large black dogs with red, fiery eyes came at him. He picked up an iron bar or some weapon and defended himself. He was however bitten on the ankle. Then, in terror, he woke up and realized it was a nightmare, but his ankle hurt, and when he got up in the morning he found two raw tooth-marks there. He had to seek medical care and he says that the doctor smiled in disbelief when he related the happenings. But psychic Sandra explained that this astral-travelling or O.B.E., [out of body experience] and that Jackie had actually been there and had encountered the dogs. After three and a half years he still bears the marks of the dogs teeth!

Two lions rampant standing at each side of the central shield. The shield contains two crossed crozier's or shepherds crooks, with Roman numerals or letters on either side. The left hand side read12, denoting the number 12, He can't recall the right hand side inscription. A crown surmounts the shield.

The ends of the crooks at the top were pointing outwards. In heraldry this denotes ecclesiastical authority, I.e. of a bishop or pope. A regular or inward pointing hook is of the ordinary occupation of a shepherd in the field, or of his trade.

So in this case, the crest has ecclesiastical significance, apparently. Popes and Bishops do take such insignia on elevation to office, and these may or may not incorporate their individual family crests, or parts thereof. However, a study of bishops coats-of-arms shows that they do not ever contain the lions, which therefore seem to be a secular or temporal feature. Furthermore, correspondence with Chief Herald of Ireland in Dublin fails to identify the crest, but does establish that it is not that of a Pope Pius12. So, there are mixed signals here, suggesting half secular and half ecclesiastical motifs. The mystery remains unresolved. Unclear also is whether the dream/nightmare has anything at all to do with the haunting at the Fahey's home. A further mystifying element of the dream is Jackie's belief that the big house was in . . . . Pennsylvania!!! At least it is not . . . . Transylvania!? [Drawing of the crest enclosed with photo's]

Chapter Ten

Divination—a second opinion

In order to corroborate or refute the previous psychic evidence here, a clairvoyant was engaged. His account agrees in the main with that of Sandra, but differs in specific detail.

He says that the poltergeist trouble in 1996'-'97 centred around Martha, and not around Sarah-Louise. Martha is Sarah's mother. He says that it has nothing to do with Sarah, and she is not a reincarnation, but a normal everyday child, and the events of the 1900's have nothing to do with this present case.[His account here is set in the chronological order of contributions given to this book]

There was a foetus aborted in the original farmhouse on the Fahey's house site, in the 1900's, he says. The father was a Roman Catholic clergyman, in fact . . . . an Arch-bishop!? [A bishop's clerical garb is almost identical, so Sandra's account tallies with this].

And the mother was not a nun, but the . . . mother of a nun at a later date. She was probably single at the time. This, too, tallies well with Sandra's account.

The foetus was aborted, on the order of the Archbishop, presumably so as to avoid religious scandal.

Sandra's vision was a symbolic resume, he says, and remarkably accurate for a quick scan. The two accounts concur then in general, and this has to be significant for the veracity of the background events, even though the clairvoyant says that they are unrelated?

He says that the disturbances of 1996-97, were centred around Martha, not her baby. Martha would have been sub-consciously, but not consciously aware, and was not a voluntary agent in the events at her home in 1996-97.

Martha is in her 20's and about four years ago she learned that she is not the daughter of Jackie and Esther Fahey, but a niece of Esther's. Her father, amazingly, is/was a relative of the archbishop, the clairvoyant say!? And uncannily, the latter was not told of Martha's situation, so he may be right!

This was the trigger, perhaps, for the poltergeist happening of '96-97, subconsciously, according to the clairvoyant. But could be mistaken about Martha's father? It is true that Martha's did have a relationship with a man, but later became ill and couldn't take care of her baby—Martha. What is difficult to accept, however, is his assertion that the 1996 events are unconnected with those of the 1900's. To the Fahey's and this writer this just can't be a matter of coincidence. The haunting of the 1900's were also of poltergeist nature, and both houses stood on exactly the same site. There simply has to be a connection!

Could Martha then be the reincarnation of the lost child of the archbishop and the nun's mother? And not her daughter Sarah-Louise?

Cry From Beyond

The clairvoyant says no she is not the reincarnation, but then, astoundingly, he repeats that Martha's father was/is . . . . a relative of the archbishop?

Thus the resemblance, presumably? And assuredly also the connection between the two separate family haunting?

He says; No connection. At least not directly. But the coincidences here are too great, surely;?

[a] that the two fathers were related;

[b] that the same house-site was the location for separate families and events and times.

This is just impossible to grasp, or believe!

If Martha had lived elsewhere, then perhaps, but the fact that she came to live on the very site of a previous haunting and that her father is/was a relative of the father in the original case. It is simply implausible, if not downright impossible, for the two events to be unrelated.

Surely the clairvoyant is mistaken here. In divining he has to ask a question and gets a YES or a No answer;

[a] Could he have confused; nun, the mother with nuns mother in regard to the maternity of the foetus? And Martha's paternity?

[b] Is he wrong in claiming no connection between the two events of 1906 and 1996?

If he right, however, in claiming Martha's paternal parentage to be related to the archbishop, then evidently that must confirm a connection between the two events of the 1900's and the 1990's.

This simply has to be the logical and reasonable conclusion. That is; that the two events are related.

This, too, would corroborate the clairvoyant's assertion that Martha was the centre of the events at her house in 1996. And it would prove the connection with 1906, if she is in fact a relative of the archbishop's. Indeed, if the clairvoyant deems t so, then he must be contradicting himself if he says that there is no connection. By the law of logic there cannot be a connection and no connection at the same time. Yet, he is remarkably accurate otherwise, and his findings concur with Sandra's in the main.

But what an amazing coincidence that two separate and distinct families would, by circuitous routes, come to occupy the same site, at different times, and be connected through a common occurrence and paternity?

Perhaps Martha would have effected a haunting experience even if she had lived elsewhere, and in whatever house she inhabited? What an astounding coincidence then that she came to live in a place connected with a relative and an event!

But would Martha have effected a haunting wherever she lived? Most likely not! Her discovery of her true parentage, though traumatic, would hardly warrant such awful events as those of '96-97. Many, many others share with her that discovery.

Cry From Beyond

The killing of a baby and a religious scandal could, however, instigate sinister reactions, in that place. It would seem, therefore, that it was the place rather than the person [Martha] that was the prime mover, in 1996-'97. But then, why was the spirit dormant for years, until Martha brought her baby home?

If Martha were the sole source of the troubles, she would surely be conscious of the fact. Esther Fahey, her adoptive mother, says that she is a most generous girl and would never bring about such terrible trails on her own relatives and home. While she was strangely, less traumatically affected by the disturbances at her home, she was unaware of her part therein. At times she too was scared, but on the whole was aloof.

Since the clairvoyant names her as the centre of the events of 1996-'97, it would seem that she may have been the agent provocateur that triggered the recurrence of the cycle of 1906. By bringing her baby into the same spot wherein a baby was aborted 90 years before, she must have unwittingly re-enacted those previous events, especially if she is a relative of the father-figure thereof.

To claim that the two eras we unconnected is surely unreasonable, especially if it is admitted that Martha and the archbishop were connected. That would be a contradiction and a false syllogism. The clairvoyant endeavours to explain the paradox later. [see his own account]. Or could he be completely mistaken about Martha altogether?

Psychic Sandra said that the nun was the mother of the child/foetus. This, perhaps, is the more plausible scenario. Firstly, an archbishop would be more likely to have dealing with a nun [n schools, parish works, etc.] than with a lay woman, living in Galway city. Unless she were a young unmarried woman, away from home?

And secondly, would it have been necessary to kill the child/foetus if the mother were a married woman: she could have passed it off as being her own? Unless she were a widow? Even then she could have had the child adopted—and far less sensationally than if a nun had done so. But again she may have been young and single bat the time. Such drastic measures as abortion/ killing, especially in those God-fearing, dread-full days, does suggest desperate, dire straits indeed-such as those of a . . . nun with child! Yet the clairvoyant is adamant that it was a lay woman, who later had a daughter a nun?

Finally, the four archbishopric Sees of Ireland are not situated anywhere near Galway city, the presumed domicile of the nun's mother. A nun, on the other hand, is invariably stationed away from home. But a young lay woman could also have been away?

Chapter Eleven

Similitude

The magazine Ireland's own features a true ghost story in every issue, in the column; Stranger than fiction, by John Macklin. The following is a resume of three of these articles which bear some resemblance to the Fahey's story. Indeed, the first one concerns a Fahey, also;

[1] The Voice in the Candle Flame-

Throughout the winter and spring of 1920, Pat Fahey, a 12 year old boy, astonished and mystified the world of physical research by receiving what he claimed were messages from the dead—through a candle flame!

Pat, from a Dublin city suburb, held that the communication were from his twin brother who died two years earlier in a bus accident, aged 10. His name was Donal. Their mother, Mrs. Bridget Fahey, was to recall that it all began after Christmas 1919 as the family sat for their evening meal by candle light.

I saw Pat looking at the flame in a strange way. Then he said that Uncle David would visit. An hour later David did call, unexpectedly, as he was living in London. How did you know, I asked Pat. Donal must have told me, he said.

Afterwards, whenever a candle was lit he would hear what he claimed was Donal's voice. As twins they had been very close. The messages would include advance notice of imminent death of people in our neighbourhood, etc.'

Pat Fahey began to hold séances for the benefit of people concerned about loved ones departed. One such person was a Mrs. Mary O'Brien, from Cork, who had lost her father, she relates; 'The moment Pat lit the candle a strange atmosphere entered the room. I could hear the voice of a boy, coming, it seemed, from the candle, relaying various messages. Everything it said about my deceases father was absolutely true. I felt comforted and reassured as to his welfare.'

By April, 1920, the "voice in the candle" was beginning to fade. At the last séance, on April 19, Donal's voice, now a whisper, was heard for the last time. It said; "I am going on a long journey but we will be together in 20 years from now." Then the candle flame flickered and died.

The years passed and Pat resumed a normal life. In 1939, at the age of 31, he joined the British Army. In April 1949, he was killed in action in Norway with the ill-fated British expeditionary force—20 years to the day after his brother's prediction via—The voice in the candle flame!"

In our Fahey family case, little Sarah continually spoke of the 'man in the bulb' or the baby in bulb. Proof it seems that earthly energy sources are utilised by the spiritual world, but where was Donal Fahey during his contacts with his brother? Was he in Purgatory, or in Limbo waiting for a reincarnation? What was the long journey he spoke of?

Because he said; 'We will meet again in 20 years time' it suggests that Donal was not reincarnated, as the meeting was obviously to be in the next life. As a mere 10 year old when he died he would not have had any great sins to expiate in Purgatory. A sojourn of two years in our terms might seem an appropriate period of purification. The long journey then may have been to Heaven, but surely the release to Heaven is an instantaneous one, and could he meet his brother, if Pat had to go first go to Purgatory for purification? Perhaps the meeting would be a spiritual communication across the divide between the two states, Heaven and Purgatory? But can a 12 year old merit entry into Heaven? A blow to the theory of reincarnation perhaps!?

[2] The Mystery of the sobbing Child;

Joyce Scarman was woken at 3a.m. by the sound of a child sobbing somewhere in the bedroom. It was July 1955, in Norwood, South London. She and her husband Geoffrey had moved into their Victorian house just four days before.

In the morning Joyce examined the room and felt drawn to the wardrobe. She sensed an overwhelming air of sadness there, the sort of feeling you get as a child when you are in a situation with which you can't cope; suffocating and terrifying.

That night the sobbing returned Joyce got out of the bed and went to the wardrobe. She recognised her concern as a maternal feeling towards whoever was making the piteous sounds. She instinctively sensed that the child felt trapped so she left the wardrobe door open and softly spoke to it in a reassuring way. The whole atmosphere in the room then changed, becoming warm and relaxed. From then on they no longer heard the sobbing.

But Joyce couldn't forget the child. Several weeks later she made contact with the previous owner, an elderly lady, who related the following;

"When we were little my sister and I had a cruel governess who would lock us in the wardrobe as punishment for trivial or imagined misdemeanour. My sister suffered greatly, becoming nervous and claustrophobic and she died at the age of 11 years old, I believe, due to this."

This case has resonances with the Fahey's story. A child died, and there's that sense of trauma and suffocation and violence and injustice. This would tend to enforce the belief that ghosts or poltergeists do not visit a house gratuitously or fortuitously, but because of a particular violent or unpleasant experience in the past. Therefore it would appear that the Fahey's experience is connected with the smothering of an infant or the aborting of a foetus in a house on the site 90 years before, and triggered anew by a new baby's arrival.

[3]   The Curse of the wronged wife

'John Houston, a wealthy brewer, of Devon and Somerset, died in the spring of 1857. He had left his property to this second wife, a marriage of four years duration, but a solicitor declared the hand written will invalid, and relatives of his first marriage claimed ownership of the property.

At 35, Maria Houston was 30 years younger than her late husband, and she felt outraged at the injustice of her loss, given the intention of his will in her favour. She cursed the property all those who deprived her of her inheritance. She died from typhoid soon after. What followed over the years was a litany of fires, farmyard animals deaths, injuries, illnesses and accidents. Owners came and went, conscious of the ill-fortune surrounding the estate of Combe House. For nearly 100 years the unhappy events intruders. There was tapping of windows, banging of walls, slamming of doors, footsteps on stairs, and items being thrown about.

The children of one family there, a Col. Butler, in the 1930's, repeatedly vacated, following persistent banging, mysterious fires, plants failures and the violent deaths of farm stock. Even an exorcism failed to bring peace to the house. Maria Houston was holding firm, it would seem. Finally, in November 1947, Combe house was entirely engulfed in a blazing inferno, the cause of which was mysterious, as it was vacant derelict.

As onlookers gathered to watch firemen fight the blaze, they remarked on seeing a strange woman in a long, flowing gown, standing apart, watching the house being destroyed . . . and smiling! She had claimed her inheritance!

Here again we see a haunting with a cause, a source, an instigator, a prime-mover. Not a chance, random or accidental occurrence. It would seem then that such events are based on actual, empirical, historical and concrete happenings having previously occurred, on those same sites. And human will or spirit. As the driving force. And this case shows both a noisy poltergeist and visible ghost phenomenon in the one event.

The Fahey's experience then must, assuredly, be based on a prior cause, and human mind, will or spirit, and it doesn't seem to matter whether the effect is a ghost or a poltergeist. Haunting then do seem to have a reason, cause and source are not inexplicable, random, mindless, chance occurrences, but is the person's spirit present in the second coming, or is it just like a photographic record replayed, like an echo or shadow of the real event?

This snippet from Irelands Own, After 2000 concerns the appearance of Roman soldiers in York. After 2000 years this is hardly an actual, real life here and now presentation; what would be the point? Therefore it must be a photographic re-echo or playback or shadow of the real events, but the soldiers or their spirits would not actually be present there, here and now? This must mean that in many cases at least, the person/spirit is not actually present in a visible ghost. So, the Shakespearean term "shade" [shadow] was probably an accurate description for example, Anne Boleyn's ghost still appears, after 450 years. But surely this is more shadow than substance, more like a reflection in a mirror, still lingering in the ethereal atmosphere. This, too, may explain why visible ghosts often don't seem to see or be aware of the real life person beholding them. The ghost is literally in a world of his own, and not really there at all, but merely the shadow of his former self. Sandra says that ghosts are harmless, and if people did realise that they are "not really there at all", there would be no need to be afraid.

Poltergeist, however, are a different phenomenon. This is a non-visual, psycho-kinetic activity, seemingly, requiring an act of intellect, mind or will, not necessarily of someone there present, but more immediate in time tan visual ghosts, usually.

Chapter Twelve

Ghost or Poltergeist

In this book; Physical Research [1910] Sir W.F. Barrett dealt with the different types of haunting, he shows that such phenomena were know to the Greeks and Romans, and he quotes Pliny and Tacitus.

In general, ghosts are visible and silent, or audible in a non-destructive or non-violent way.

Poltergeist, however, are invisible, but noisy and violent or mischievous, as in the Fahey's home. Mr. Barrett elaborates;

Poltergeist's

We have no exact English equivalent for the German word "Poltergeist", usually translated "hobgoblin", a "paltered" in German is a noisy or boisterous fellow, and a "poltergeist" is, therefore, a boisterous ghost. The phenomena are sporadic, breaking out suddenly and disappearing after a few weeks or months. Unlike ghosts, the disturbances appear to gather around a particular, usually young, person, in a particular place. Objects are thrown, furniture moved, noises made, all utterly meaningless. And the closest scrutiny fails to discover any explanation or obvious cause.

One of the best attested English cases occurred in 1661 and is known as the Demon or Drummer of Tedworth. This case was examined by fellows of the Royal Society. The facts are as follows; The magistrate of Tedworth, Wilts. Ordered the arrest of the vagrant drummer; shortly afterwards at the magistrate's house began an amazing series of noises and disturbances which continued for two years. The drummer was tried for witchcraft but was acquitted, and the disturbances continued even when he was far way in jail or at times when he was otherwise occupied.

It was observed that all of the phenomena were centred around the magistrate's two young children, who were oblivious to the events, and had nothing to do with the drummer'—W.F. Barrett.

While this case demonstrates an apparent connection between the events in the house and the magistrate's arrest of the drummer, it must be pointed out that almost all of the other cases cited by Mr. Barrett show no logical explanation whatsoever, as to cause or effect, and perhaps even in this case, it could be a matter of chance or coincidence. Interesting, too, that young children were involved, and innocently so.

It would appear, however, that the drummer somehow, consciously or subconsciously, caused the disturbances in the magistrate's house, possibly out of a sense of grievance at his arrest. But why were the children involved?

Could this be similar to the Fahey case? Baby Sarah-Louise was centrally involved but totally innocent, according to both our psychic and clairvoyant. But could we substitute Martha for the drummer?

Both of our experts named Martha as the prime-mover of events at her home, however, unwittingly on her part.

Martha never knew her father and was adopted at 10 weeks old by her aunt and uncle-in-law, Esther and Jackie Fahey. She may have been psychologically affected thereby and have felt deprived. And if her father was a relative of the archbishop of the 1906 case with its own attendant poltergeist events, is it not likely then that simply events would occur again, as in 1996? Especially as the very same site is common to both! To say, like the clairvoyant that the two events are unrelated, is simply too much of a coincidence, if not downright unbelievable. And there surely must be a cause and a reason for poltergeists, and their manifestation in certain houses only. [see the third Ireland's own story. This story demonstrates a combination of ghost and poltergeist].

The clairvoyant [who wishes to remain anonymous] contributes his own explanation of paranormal phenomena here;

Poltergeists

Poltergeists manifest in many ways, e.g., doors open and close, objects are thrown about, and noises come from all over the house. Furniture items move on their own. Telephones and electrical apparatus are particularly vulnerable, often shattering or melting. Objects are flung across the room, but rarely strike anyone. However, there are cases where people were pinched, bitten, and even sexually assaulted.

The activities start and stop abruptly. They may last from periods of hours to months, occasionally for years. Disturbances occur mainly at night, and in all recorded cases a young female between early teens and early twenties lives in the house.

She is not consciously aware of being the centre of the disturbances, and remains aloof and detached. She may be inwardly pleased with the affect she is having, however.

In his book Psychical Research, Sir. William Barrett, and William Roll of the Psychical Research Foundation, identified patterns peculiar to these phenomena, which they labelled; Recurrent Spontaneous Psycho-Kinesis [R.S.P.K.]. That is, inexplicable, spontaneous physical effects. Researchers have found that there is a common denominator associated with poltergeist activity;

[1] The female is in the early stages of puberty; or

[2] she is a sexually repressed teenager, or

[3] she is a pregnant girl, aged 15 to 25.

In almost all cases there was sexual repression or guilt. With the girl suffering an acute anxiety state, mania, or stress. In some cases mental illness was diagnosed. Where therapy and counselling were given, the poltergeist activity ceased. [Sandra's healing, in the Fahey case?]

Poltergeist activity is not confined to any country or century. In both ancient and modern literature, accounts of poltergeists are recorded. E.g., Pliny, Tacitus, even the bible, and today, worldwide. Nothing new, then what is new, however, is that there is an awareness now that the sub-conscious part of the brain is an untapped reservoir of power, capable of performing great feats, through a process we call

Telekinesis, I.e., the ability to move animate and inanimate objects with the power of thought alone.

At the time when this power is released there is deep emotional disturbance in the person at will and, indeed, move mountains.

There is no other explanation, I believe, for the events in the Fahey household in Galway. Talk of similar happenings in an old farmhouse which once to do with recent events. Past events have left their own imprint on the site, but I believe that the two cases are not directly connected. There may well have been haunting in the past and there are strong lye-lines and water channels there, which give off a form of radiation that ascends in a pillar-like formation. These are know as cold spots and can be measured by a magnetometer.

These lye-lines and other conditions, such as fog and murky and half light gloom, can accentuate the conditions conducive to seeing ghosts. Apart from the lye-lines, possibly, these conditions have no relationship, I believe, to the poltergeist activity at the Fahey home, however.

When the emotions and the logical part of the brain become balanced in the person [expedited by counselling], harmony reigns, eventually, and the poltergeist phenomena then cease.

Jonathan Fahey

Clairvoyant.

N.B.;

The Fahey case is not just of a poltergeist, but is a ghost-story as well.

Sarah-Louise today describes seeing 'the man in the bulb', and the "the baby".

She says that the man was "bold", and that the baby was not "a real baby" but floated around the room, and played with her toys.

And there was a third apparition, the young girl in the hall in white clothes. Jackie's sister died at 12 years of age, just after her Confirmation.

Four Today

Sarah-Louise is Four today,
Bright and chirpy as a bird,
Doing chores around the house,
For this is what I've heard.

Mammy's busy, Granny works,
So Sarah says "Hello"!
Into the phone, to take her calls,
From those who love her, ... So!

She knows the voices, and to each one,
She tells of all she's got; [presents];
A dress from 'Tricia, and many more,
Although she's just . . . . a Tot!

Sarah will soon be big
But we'll always think of how,
She was such a happy, bubbly, chatty child,
And beautiful, then . . . . as now!

-For her birthday
On 28th of September 2000.

Conclusion

All is peaceful and quite on the western front at the Fahey home today, in 2000 A.D. The family have recovered gradually, and their home is warm and friendly once again. The two central characters in the drama, Martha and Sarah-Louise, have moved to their own house now. Martha has found a new, loving, secure relationship and plans to marry in vivacious child; happy, intelligent and independent.

All's well that ends well, so rightly seethe the bard!, but what can be said of this true-life drama now, with the benefit of hindsight vision?

The two psychic experts involved in the story agree on the essential details of the prior events, of the 1900's. A child/foetus was conceived/born to an Bishop/ Archbishop and a nun/or mother of, and was aborted/killed. The psychic involved in healing the Fahey home, Sandra, believes that the events of the 1900's instigated the attack of 1996-'97, through the sub-conscious agency of Martha [and Sarah-Louise?] Fahey.

The clairvoyant ascribes only an indirect relationship between the two events, and declares Martha to be the sole, unwitting instigator, in her own case. The two expert agree also that neither Martha nor Sarah-Louise are reincarnations.

What do the Fahey's and this writer think? We acknowledge the expertise of both psychics and we would accept whichever case that were proven. But in the absence thereof, we tend to learn in Sandra's favour. It was, she after all, who "saw" and healed the spirit-baby, Martha and the Fahey home.

Given the reality of the eggshells and the smell of rotting flesh, we see an inevitable connection with the dead foetus/ baby of the 1900's. However, we do recognise that it was Martha's arrival with her baby which initiated the disturbances in 1997. But surely it would be too great a coincidence if the two events were unrelated, given that the two men were related!

Finally, Jackie Fahey has an interesting intuition. He suggests that if, indeed, Martha's Father was a close relative of the archbishop's, then the spirit of the first baby returned to protect Sarah from a possible similar fate to that suffered by himself, circa 1906. And here too, the clairvoyant's opinion would come into play; If Martha, in a temporary and insecure relationship, had unintentionally became pregnant, and was, therefore, confused, disturbed and unhappy, she may subconsciously and un wittingly and unknowingly, have resented, rejected and even denied her baby's existence. It is to Martha's eternal credit that she did not terminate her pregnancy or her child's life, as happened in the original case, in that terrible battle of spirits.

Her reward? The beautiful and gifted child—Sarah-Louise, so treasured and beloved, by all today-and forever!

Amen.

Microcosmopolitan

Life after death in Corrib Park

—By—
Richard Chapman

I WAS disappointed to read that the Corrib Park poltergeist has been exorcised before there was any serious investigation. (No, I don't call the Herald sending that reporter serious investigation). Why is there so little interest in putting these things under a microscope? There's so much to be found out here, so many questions. To take an example, I find it interesting that the ghost of a baby can move a TV set around, whereas a live one cannot. What does that mean?

Exposure

Or, why did nobody get round with a camcorder? Despite film and sound recording having been in existence for over a century, there is little or nothing in the way of recorded evidence of poltergeist activity. And while it seems likely that spiritual manifestation would not be photographable—and this disinclines me to believe in photographs which purport to be of ghosts even more than the fact that they generally appear to be double exposures—things flying around a room certainly are. Is it cynical to think that such footage is so much rarer simply because you can tell when something is being hurled cross the room by the agency of a bit of fishing line.

I don't believe it's just that people are too scared. I for one would be entirely happy to spend a night in a haunted house, and I'm sure many others would too. (Come to think of it, there was a business opportunity here). Genuine ghosts are hard to come by these days. I guess this is just another sign of declining spiritual values. That's why it's so amazing when one of such high quality as this comes along. Not just the ghost of a murdered baby, but the ghost of a murdered baby whose mother was a nun, *and* whose father was a priest. That's incredible.

Lurid

I mean, litereally. Quite why does the story have to be so lurid? I'm sure the circumstances didn't make much of a difference to the ghost's unhappiness. No, I'm afraid I don't find the medium's version of events terribly convincing. At all.

But doubt is an entirely different thing from disproof. Some people don't believe in ghosts, some do. Many claim to have personal experience of them, and while you don't want to dismiss anybody's sincerely-held belief, we do all hallucinate and perceive things incorrectly from time to time. In fact, it does not seem scientific to just *ignore* a phenomenon so widely reported. Here was a golden opportunity to put video surveillance cameras in every room, and actually *see* the baby clothes, toys and pictures being moved. Nothing could have been easier. Why did nobody care enough to fo to this litle trouble?

The ultimate question

It is after all about the most important question we can ever ask or hope to answer. If ghosts exist, then that confirms the existence of life after death. I think that's worth knowing for sure, to say the least.

But before anybody gets a chance to investigate properly, the ghost gets exorcised. What a terrible waste of an opportunity. Let's not let it happen again.

☐ **SMASHED: Jackie Fahy with a jug broken** hours — and the others now followed suit, vowing never to spend another night in their home of 25 years.

The night was now really starting to get to me. Even the most banal stuffed toy was beginning to assume a sinister aspect. Had that cute turtle on the sideboard really worn such a menacing leer earlier on?

Think haunted houses, and it's usually crumbling castles awash with turrets and parapets that spring to mind, rather than the tidy terraced council abode that was the Fahy's home until this morning.

Inside the doors of No 286 Corrib Park, the smart new fitted kitchen and hand stencilled poppies on the living room wall paint a picture of cosy suburban bliss.

But the sunken eyes and tearstained cheeks of mother Esther Fahy tell a different story.

"That's it, we're gone. I can't live here anymore with these things happening. I don't care where we go, it's driving me insane," she said, even before the worst of the night's events had unfolded.

A baby's cotton pinny lying in the centre of her grandchilds bedroom was the immediate cause of her anguish.

Moments earlier the garment had been lying neatly folded on a locker — but when I followed Martha Fahy (21) and her brother Michael (25) into the room it had mysteriously jumped yards away to the centre of the floor.

SPOOKY

As if on cue eight-month-old baby Sarah Louise who had been sleeping peacefully in her pram downstairs awoke with a piercing cry of distress.

Like her grandmother the baby was inconsolable — and had to be brought next door to the neighbours who have thrown open their doors to the family.

Every major incident in the house this last week has been heralded by the baby's uncharacteristic wails which stop abruptly as soon as she brought away from the scene.

Following a Mass on Wednesday evening the family had hoped the eerie events would cease but all

☐ **ARRIVING SCEPTICAL: Aideen Sheehan** they got that night was a few hours fitful sleep huddled together in the living room for safety. Last night even that was denied them.

The crucifixes, Mass cards and copious quantities of Holy Water which friends and wellwishers have lavished upon the family were lined up on the sideboard but were proving sadly ineffectual last night.

"The priest blessed every cupboard, and every corner of the house, even the attic. We really hoped that would be the end of the whole saga," said family head Jackie who works as a driver for the Brothers of Charity.

The family are the first and only inhabitants of the Corrib Park house — there is no previous owner on which to pin the blame for the possibly paranormal events.

Jackie said they were desperately trying to investigate if any tragic deaths had occurred in the area before their estate was built.

"There was a farm house behind where the house is now, and we think there could have been a sudden death around there of a child or young mother that might explain what's going on now. If we could find out we might be able to pray for that soul to be put to rest so this would end," he said.

UNNATURAL

A psychic who had had a similar experience previously had been in touch with them and they are now hoping she might be able to tackle the problem.

But given everything the family have experienced they didn't think they will ever be able to sleep peacefully in the house again, Michael said.

"When I first arrived I was frankly disbelieving as family members claimed to hear footsteps from the bedroom upstairs.

I didn't imagine that violently smashed ornament or displaced furniture — and I'm still trying to come up with any rational explanation.

EXCLUSIVE
TO ALL STORES FROM TODAY
CHAMPION SPORTS
IRELANDS NO.1 SPORTS & FITNESS STORES
DUBLIN, LIMERICK, GALWAY

a bump in the night

☐ CLEARING UP: Michael Fahy picking up the pieces from the china dog early today

☐ UNEXPLAINED: Aideen Sheehan and Michael Fahy examine the broken china dog

Lightning Source UK Ltd.
Milton Keynes UK
UKOW04f0202140214

226455UK00002B/131/P